Red Wind Crossing

Also by John D. Nesbitt
in Large Print:

Black Diamond Rendezvous
Coyote Trail
Man from Wolf River
One-Eyed Cowboy Wild
Wild Rose of Ruby Canyon
North of Cheyenne

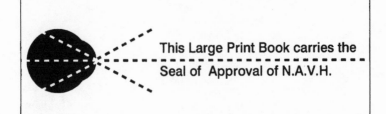

This Large Print Book carries the
Seal of Approval of N.A.V.H.

Red Wind Crossing

John D. Nesbitt

Thorndike Press • Waterville, Maine

Published in 2004 by arrangement with Leisure Books,
a division of Dorchester Publishing Co., Inc.

Thorndike Press® Large Print Western.

The tree indicium is a trademark of Thorndike Press.

The text of this Large Print edition is unabridged.
Other aspects of the book may vary from the original edition.

Set in 16 pt. Plantin by Minnie B. Raven.

Printed in the United States on permanent paper.

Library of Congress Cataloging-in-Publication Data

Nesbitt, John D.
    Red wind crossing / John D. Nesbitt.
        p. cm.
    ISBN 0-7862-6443-8 (lg. print : hc : alk. paper)
    1. South Platte River Valley (Colo. and Neb.) — Fiction.
2. Large type books.   I. Title.
PS3564.E76R44 2004
813'.54—dc22   2004047929

For the girls of Chihuahua

As the Founder/CEO of NAVH, the only national health agency solely devoted to those who, although not totally blind, have an eye disease which could lead to serious visual impairment, I am pleased to recognize Thorndike Press★ as one of the leading publishers in the large print field.

Founded in 1954 in San Francisco to prepare large print textbooks for partially seeing children, NAVH became the pioneer and standard setting agency in the preparation of large type.

Today, those publishers who meet our standards carry the prestigious "Seal of Approval" indicating high quality large print. We are delighted that Thorndike Press is one of the publishers whose titles meet these standards. We are also pleased to recognize the significant contribution Thorndike Press is making in this important and growing field.

Lorraine H. Marchi, L.H.D.
Founder/CEO
NAVH

★ Thorndike Press encompasses the following imprints: Thorndike, Wheeler, Walker and Large Pr int Press.

Chapter One

Red Wind Crossing lies on the South Platte River as it spills out of the Rockies and heads for the plains of Colorado. A fellow might not guess how the place got its name if he didn't happen to pass by when the wind was blowing. I've been there more times than I could tell, but on one of my first visits I got a hint as to why it has the name of Red Wind. On the south side of the river, back about a hundred yards or so, a red cutbank rises to the height of a man on horseback. I had just come up from the river, where I had washed a shirt, and I was in the process of shaking it out when a gust of wind blew up from the east. All of a sudden the air was full of that powdery dirt, and it looked like a red wind.

I remember holding up my wet shirt and seeing it was all speckled. It looked like someone had worn it for an afternoon of killing chickens, which I sure hadn't. I don't care to be around a chicken when it has had its head cut off and is flapping around, spraying blood. When I got big enough to ride a horse, I left it to someone else to tend to the dead chickens.

Of course, I don't care to be around dead men, either. They tend to show up in the wrong places, at the wrong times, and the men you think would have been more deserving are safe in a nice house, counting their money or sipping expensive wine or lording it over a good-looking woman who doesn't smile much. That's what's wrong with dead men, or at least the ones a fellow stumbles across. There's usually something wrong. That's the way it was with Jimmy Rooks.

I was supposed to meet him one day at Red Wind Crossing, and I got there first, or so I thought. It being a warm August afternoon, I dismounted and led my horse to the water's edge where he could drink. There aren't any trees right there at the crossing, just rocks and scrub brush on the hillsides, so I moved my horse around to where he cast a good shadow in front of him, and I sat down to wait for my pal.

The day seemed open and easy enough as I rested there with my knees up in front of me and my arms hooked around them, the reins of my horse trailing over my right shoulder and snugged in my right hand. I watched the river flow by, nice and calm. I thought about a mug of cold beer, a sizzling steak being lifted from the skillet, a dark-haired girl laughing. I suppose those are normal thoughts for a young fellow who spends most of his time on dusty trails and in cobwebbed line shacks. I know they've always been normal thoughts for me.

Not too long after I sat down I caught the movement of a bird soaring out over the river. I tipped my head up and saw it was a buzzard, circling back above the rocks that lay behind me and to my left. I didn't think much of it at first, but after he made a few more passes I started to feel uneasy. I can tell when I'm squinting too hard, and that's what I was doing, so I pushed myself up onto my feet and looked around.

I didn't see anyone or any movement at all. Then I looked up and saw the buzzard still floating on the air. I thought, *I'll go take a look in those rocks while I'm waiting.* So I did, and that's where I found my friend sprawled out, bare-headed and mouth open, with a bullet hole in his chest.

It was my saddle pard, Jimmy Rooks, about as good a friend as a fellow is likely to have in the life we led. He was the other Jimmy in our little bunch. Now there was only one of us — me, Jimmy Clevis — and I was wondering if something had caught up with my namesake. And the next logical thought was that if something had come looking for him, it might come after me.

There was no telling what might have led someone to do it. Jimmy Rooks was a fun-loving young man, sometimes a little reckless. I didn't know what-all might have lurked in his past. I had heard him say more than once that he didn't care if he ever went back to "Missoura," so maybe someone from there followed him out here, though I didn't think so. Maybe it was something that came straight from the kind of work we had been doing — throwing the wide loop. Then again, maybe it was something else he'd been up to lately and I didn't know about. For as little as he talked about his early days, he gave the impression that he didn't have any unfinished business back home. Now I wondered if he had any other affairs in his life, more recent, that he didn't get to tend to.

This was what it came to, I thought. I could remember him as I'd seen him so many times — hat tipped back, brown hair falling over his forehead, brown eyes shining as he laughed. Telling jokes in the Jack-Deuce, drinking straight out of the bottle at a line camp. Jimmy was a good one. As for honor among thieves, as the saying went, he was sterling. But someone saw fit to put a bullet through him and dump him here in the rocks, where he lay with dirt in his hair. I could make out horse tracks at the edge of the rocks, and I could see the marks on the ground where someone had dragged the body. Whoever had done it had shot him somewhere else and brought him here. I wondered why someone would kill him at all, and I couldn't help wondering what, if anything, it meant for me.

I stood there by Jimmy for a little while, not looking straight at him but not feeling that I could just walk away. I didn't know what to do next. The standard thing to do when someone finds a dead person is to report it, but Jimmy and I and the bunch we ran with didn't have the habit of going to the law. And I hadn't been at it long enough with these fellows to know whether we buried our own.

If I had known who killed him I would have had a better idea of what to do. I didn't think this was done from the inside, because Jimmy was true to the code. So it must have been from the outside, and from the way he had been disposed of, it didn't seem like vigilante work. Those fellows either left the body where it fell or left it out in the open as a warning. So he must have been done in for some other reason, which to my way of thinking made it into a case of a regular citizen being killed by an unknown hand. As much as I winced at the thought, it seemed like something that should be turned over to the law.

For a little while I was stuck there, not knowing how to go about it. I didn't like the idea of riding into town to the sheriff's office, then riding back out with him, and answering a thousand questions. On the other hand, I couldn't just ride away and leave my friend to the buzzards. Then it occurred to me that if the news got to the sheriff at second or third hand, it might take some of the edge off of it and keep me out of the center of things.

With that thought in my mind I rode upriver the mile or so to Mexican town, which lies on the south side of the river, across from the main part of town. Monetta isn't all that big, but the part that has the bank, the post office, the hotel, the boardinghouse, and the sheriff's office — in other words, the white part — keeps to its own side of the river. I get along well enough on either side, and for right now I liked the side I was on.

When I got to the edge of the little *colonia*, as they call it, I could smell woodsmoke. To me that meant some of the women had their cookstoves going, and I could imagine the warm, toasty smell of tortillas coming off the stovetop. I thought about how nice it was, at this time of day, to be sitting in a Mexican house, being offered a hot flour tortilla, and spreading some butter on it and maybe some salt. Then I remembered the business I came on, and I decided I had better save that pleasure for another day.

I thought the best way to pass on the information would be to have one person tell another, so I kept an eye out for a *chavalo*. I had that word running through my mind because it meant a kid, and my notion of the word was a kid old enough to go get a bucket of beer or take a message to a girl who lived in thus-and-such a house. When I saw one I called out to him, and he came over to the road. He was about eleven or twelve. I spoke to him in Spanish.

"Your name is Carlos, isn't it?"

"Yes."

"You know me?"

"Yes. Yimi."

That's how they pronounce Yeemee, with the sounds clipped short. "That's right," I said. "Now, look. I have to go to the ranch, so I don't have much time. But I want you to go tell Chanate — you know he's my friend — that down at the crossing there is a dead man. In the rocks, on this side of the river. Someone gave him a bullet. He was my friend, and that's how I found him. Tell Chanate that Yimi thinks the sheriff should know. And tell him I'll go see him before long, but I'm in a hurry today. All right?"

Carlos nodded.

"Good. And this is for you." I reached down and handed him a nickel.

"Thank you, Yimi."

"You're welcome. Thanks to you."

As he turned to walk toward the *colonia,* I reined my horse around and took off at a trot. I let out a long breath. That part was over. Even though I did need to get back to the ranch, as I had told Carlos, I figured I had time to swing by the crossing again to see if I could find anything I'd missed the first time. And besides, I thought I could keep the buzzards off of Jimmy for a few minutes at least.

Nothing had changed while I was gone. The dark bird was still floating on the air, the sun was still shining, and the river was still flowing. The body hadn't moved, and

I saw no new tracks. I decided to ride around the area a ways to see if I could pick up any other signs, but I didn't see anything to add to what I already knew. Two horses had come from the south and had gone back that way. I imagined the second horse riding away with an empty saddle, and I thought, *A one-man job.*

I went back to the rocks and looked across the river, where I saw a rider come down the slope and head for the crossing. It looked like Turner. I waved, and he waved back. I rode down to meet him as he came up out of the water, stirrups dripping.

"What's new?" he called out.

"Nothin' good."

"Is that right?" He reined his horse in and looked straight at me. He wore a brown hat with a rattlesnake hatband and a floppy brim. It kept his face in shadow. "Somethin' happen?"

"I guess so." I motioned with my head toward the rocks. "I found Jimmy Rooks over there, with a bullet hole in him."

"Dead?"

"All the way."

He shook his head, slow, as he looked down and then back up. "The boss ain't gonna like this."

"I don't know why he would — not him or anyone else, least of all Jimmy."

Turner reached into his pants pocket, drew out his jackknife, and opened it. Then he tipped his hat back on his head, and I could see his red hair and freckled, blotchy complexion. With his left hand he brought out a plug of tobacco, which he lifted to the level of his chin. His right hand came up, with the knife blade and thumb all ready, and he cut off a quid and tucked it into his mouth. He gave it a couple of big chews, spit out some juice, and said, "What do you think we should do?"

"Well," I said, "I've already done something. I rode into Mexican town and left word for someone to go tell the sheriff."

Turner's blue eyes opened up in his face. "What the hell you wanna do somethin' like that for?"

I shrugged. "I guess I thought he deserved it."

Turner cocked his eyebrows as he reached back and put away the plug of tobacco. "Jeezechrise, Clevis. You'll have these heel flies all over us, askin' questions and pokin' their nose around." He spit again, wiped his knife on his pants leg, folded it up, and put it away.

16

"I don't think it had much to do with us. Someone killed him somewhere else and dumped him here. It came from the outside, as near as I could tell, and that makes it just like any other death for the law to look into."

Turner shook his head again. "I think you done somethin' stupid. I wouldn't've said a thing."

"What was I supposed to do? If we take him back and bury him, it looks like we did it ourselves or at least have something to hide. And I wasn't going to just leave him here."

"You could have waited to ask one of us." He lowered his hat again, a habit he had from his pink skin not taking the sun too well.

"Rudd would be the one to ask, and I didn't think I'd see him — or you either, for that matter — until I got back to the place."

"Well, I think we'd better be gittin' back there right now, if you've got the law on the way." He looked in back of him, across the river, and then at me. "Rudd's not gonna like this, and neither is the boss."

I glanced at the rocks. "Like I said, I don't think anyone would."

"Well, let's git goin'."

17

"Do you want to go take a look?"

"Who, me?" He shook his head. "I've seen dead men before, and they don't do me no good. I'll remember Jimmy the way I seen him last."

"Well, go on ahead. I'm gonna go say good-bye to him, and then I'll catch up with you."

Turner didn't say anything all the way back to the line camp, except once when he rode too close to a low-hanging pine branch and knocked his hat off. Then he said two things, to no one in particular, as he turned his horse around and stepped down to get his hat.

We rode into the line camp, which was just a shack and some corrals, in the late afternoon. About a dozen horses grazed in the pasture west of the shack. The place was an old homestead, a hundred and sixty acres, that someone had tried to make a go of. Now it was one of three or four that the boss had gotten his hands on, so he had his operation spread out. The fellows at one camp didn't know too much about what went on at the others, except that stock got moved back and forth. We didn't ask questions or see much of the boss. Our orders came through Rudd.

It looked as if all his horses were in the pasture, so I figured he was having a little snooze. As the shack faced east, the door was in shadow at that time of the day. I didn't see it open, but from one glance to the next I saw Rudd appear. He wasn't the type to show up at the door bareheaded and sock-footed, rubbing his eyes. Not Rudd. He always turned out ready, as he was now, with his narrow-brimmed black hat, his tight vest buttoned as always, and his pants tucked into his stovepipe boots. He carried his gun tied down so that it looked as if he knew how to get at it pretty fast. He smoked one of his slender cigarettes as he watched us ride in.

"Where's the other Jimmy?" he called out as we came close.

"Back at the river," said Turner.

"What the hell's he doin' there?"

"Nothin'. He's dead."

"The hell." Rudd blew away a cloud of smoke.

"Clevis found him."

Turner and I both got down from our horses.

Rudd turned his narrow gaze on me. "Is that right?"

I nodded.

"Why didn't you bring him back?"

Turner answered. "Jimmy here thought he should report it, so he sent word to the sheriff."

Rudd gave me a hard look, and his thin, bristly mustache tensed until he spoke. "You did what?"

"I went to Mexican town and sent word for someone to go report it. I thought it would be less trouble that way."

Rudd, who was a scratch above average height and got a little more from the high heels on his boots, looked down at me and made a tight smile. "You think of everything, don't you?"

"Not all at once, and not always soon enough, I guess."

"I guess. You've always got an answer, haven't you?"

I wanted to say, *You've always got a question,* but I kept quiet.

He took a drag on his cigarette and shook his head. "You're a stupid little son of a bitch."

He wasn't that much taller than I was, just enough to look down at me, but he was several years older as well, and he liked to call Jimmy and me "little," to emphasize that he gave orders and we didn't. I was used to it, and I was already getting the idea that I wasn't going to listen to it for the rest of my life, so I just stood there.

Turner spoke up. "He thinks it was an outside job."

"He thinks. He thinks. Go put your horses away."

Turner didn't say anything as we stripped the horses, brushed them down, and put them out in the pasture. After we stowed our saddles in the lean-to, I told him I would go inside later, so he left me by myself. I figured he would like a chance to tell the foreman his version and then I could take the brunt of it. At that moment I didn't care who got mad at what. I felt I had done right by Jimmy Rooks, and to hell with the rest of them.

I waited outside, watching the horses graze and looking up into the sky from time to time. Off to the west I noticed the sun starting to slip downward, and it seemed as if Turner had been inside for about half an hour. I thought he and Rudd had had enough time to work me over, so I decided to go on in.

The shack was the kind of place that a person with cleaner tendencies would call a boar's nest. It had two bunks along each of the side walls, a sheet-iron stove at the far end, and a rickety table with four chairs in the middle. Each side wall had a window covered with oiled paper, which let in a bit of feeble light but no ventilation. The place always had a smell to it, the odor of dirty clothes that lay heaped at the foot of each bunk, mixed with the smell of men who didn't bathe very often. Depending on the time of day, the background odor blended with the smells of bacon grease, fried beef, or coffee — or, like now, kerosene fumes and tobacco smoke.

Rudd and Turner sat at the table with the lamp in the middle. Both of them had taken their hats off. Rudd was stubbing out the pinched end of a cigarette as I walked in. He pushed the sardine can away from him and looked at me. I took off my hat and hung it on the wall, then sat at the table with the two of them.

Rudd gave me the hard look again. "You did something stupid, Clevis, but we're not goin' to talk about it all night. The point is, you need to learn to talk less. Two things happened that can't be changed now. One is, Jimmy got killed, and the other is, you went and told someone. That second one could have been avoided, and you need to know that. Do you understand?"

"Uh-huh."

"So we're goin' to leave it at that unless

somethin' comes of it."

I nodded. "How about the other thing?"

"What's that?"

"Jimmy Rooks and why he got killed. Can we talk about that, and who might have done it or why?"

He raised his head and turned it to give me a crosswise look. As he did so, the lantern light gave a shine to his light brown hair where it had been matted down by his hat. "Look," he said, "there's no profit in that. It's bone-pickin' at best."

"You mean, you don't care?"

Now he looked at me straight on. "I mean, it doesn't do any good to look into it too close. There's not enough in it. Jimmy probably got caught at something, and the less we know about it, and the less we poke our nose into it, the less likely it is to come back to us."

"Well, it just didn't seem like the way stockmen would do it, or a range detective either."

He gave me a backward wave of the hand. "It doesn't matter. Someone did it, and the less we know, the better."

Turner cleared his throat, and I could tell he was getting ready to sound knowledgeable. For as much as he liked to give me the silent treatment when it was just the two of us, he liked to talk, and he liked to give himself a buildup. Now that he had our attention, he reached down by his leg and hauled up a bottle of whiskey. He pulled the cork out with a squeak and offered the bottle to Rudd, who shook his head. He took a swig himself and then offered me one. I shook my head, although it wasn't a firm habit for me to turn down a drink.

He wiped his mouth with the back of his sleeve and pushed the cork back into the neck of the bottle. "Well, I'll tell you the plain and simple of it," he said. "The big mucky-mucks do as they damn well please, any way they please. You know damn well they got started out brandin' whatever they got their hands on, and even now they pay their hands so much a head for anything they can maverick. But the little man who tries to do the same thing, he's in trouble. He thinks what's good for the goose is good for the gander, and if he gets a little careless, why, that's when they get him. A fellow doesn't have to do something out-and-out wrong, just do what everyone else does, but if he's not smart enough about it, then maybe somethin' happens to him."

"Still," I said, "it just doesn't seem like the way they would do it."

"Aw, hell, they do it any way they want. Isn't that right, Axel?"

Rudd sat back in his chair and turned to one side, hiking up his right leg. "Yeah, yeah. The big mucky-mucks. I wish you'd both dry up on this thing. Ben, why don't you get a fire going, and Jimmy, why don't you start slicin' up some spuds and meat? I'll open the door to let in some fresh air. It ought to be coolin' down outside by now."

I went to work slicing potatoes and put them in a skillet that had grease left over from the morning meal. Then I cut slices of salt pork and laid them in a dry skillet. All the time I did this, I wondered how much longer I would be able to hold out at this place and how much trouble it might bring me if I tried to get away. For a fellow like myself, who usually found it easier not to worry too much about whether something was right or wrong, it seemed kind of odd to be thinking this way. I could tell it wasn't just that I was tired of Turner and Rudd, but that they were like a pot of beans that had taken on a bad taste. I realized I didn't like their outlook on things, and I didn't like being told not to think or talk about something I had a stake in.

I looked at Rudd, who was building himself another cigarette, and at Turner, who was crouched in front of the open door of the stove and poking at the fire. Yep, I thought, it might cost me a little trouble to get out of this place, but sooner or later I was going to have to.

Chapter Two

The next day was bright and clear, and I was glad to get back out on the open range. I had my usual orders to ride out and about, keep one eye peeled for anything that didn't look right, and keep the other eye open for anything that looked like an opportunity. It should have given me a free feeling to be off on my own like that, cantering along under a wide blue sky, but the idea of Jimmy Rooks lying on his back in the dark of a pine box weighed on me like a set of chains. It was hard enough to think that Jimmy would never get to see any of this again, and then on top of that I had the feeling that I might be the only person in the world who cared.

I couldn't sit easy, and I knew I wouldn't be able to until I gave a try at finding out something. I imagined the news had made its way around town by now, on both sides of the river, and if anyone had a little more knowledge of what Jimmy Rooks might have been up to, that knowledge might have worked its way into circulation. That's the way it seems to go. Someone like a banker, for example, all the time he's alive, comes off as a model citizen. But then let some disaster hit him, and the truth comes tumbling out that he abandoned a wife and children in Pennsylvania, or had fathered a child with a servant girl, or was in deep financial trouble, or had a fatal weakness for the bottle. Things that no one seemed to know before came spilling out like dirty laundry from the closet, and dark secrets became common knowledge. Jimmy wasn't a banker, but I thought his getting killed might have shaken loose some bit of information. So I cut across country at midday and rode into Monetta.

It does seem to make a certain kind of sense to me that if a fellow looks too hard for a specific thing, he'll find something else instead. That's what happened to me. I was looking for information about my dead friend, and I found a girl. I was riding down a side street and she was walking ahead on my right, and even though she gave a glance to the right in back of her, she didn't seem to be paying any attention to me.

When I see a pretty girl walking down the street and looking over her shoulder, I pay attention, especially when she's walking kind of fast. I could tell she was looking to see if anyone was following, but I also got the sense that she was searching for some person she knew.

I felt like asking her if she was looking for someone, but that's an old line, and you usually use it with girls who are standing in one place. So I asked in a different way. First I had to catch up with her, ride past, stop, and turn. Then I had my question ready.

"Is there something I can do for you?"

She stopped and let out a quick breath. "I don't know."

As the conversation hung in the air for a second, I got a good look at her. She had blond hair, blue eyes, and a nice shape beneath the long, pale cotton dress. She looked to be in her early twenties — not fresh off the farm, but not yet wise to all of the ways of the world.

She looked over her shoulder again and then forced a smile as she looked back at me.

"Is there someone after you?"

"No, not really."

"Well, if there's something I can do, don't be afraid to mention it." I caught myself giving her a roving glance, so I held steady on her eyes and said, "My name's Jimmy Clevis."

She seemed to flinch and recover at the same time, and I wondered if she had heard something not so favorable about me.

"My name is Helen," she said. "Helen Garry."

"It's nice to meet you. I don't believe I've seen you before."

"No, I don't think so."

"Are you new here?"

She frowned. "Not really. I just don't get out much."

I swung down from my horse. "Well, like I said, if there's anything I can —"

"Um, I don't think so. I'm just out on a little walk, and I really shouldn't be talking to anyone."

Now it was my turn to frown. "So there *is* someone on the lookout for you."

Her face took on a pained look. "Please. You're very kind, and it's nice to meet you, but I think you should ride on."

"Well, I don't want to make you uncomfortable." I put my left foot in the stirrup and then paused to look at her.

"It's not that," she said.

"Maybe we'll see each other again sometime, then."

Her face relaxed. "Maybe so."

I swung aboard and gathered my reins,

then gave her a wink. "So long, Helen. Take care of yourself."

"Oh, I will. There's nothing to worry about there."

I moved my horse forward and did not look back at her, and before I had gone twenty yards I was glad I had kept myself from gawking. For up ahead on my left, an older woman had just come around the corner and was walking after the girl. She was moving at a fast pace, pushing herself, or so it seemed from the way she was breathing. In her left hand she carried a ring of keys that jingled as she passed me.

I caught a quick look at her, and it almost gave me a fright. She had a powdery face surrounded by medium-length, reddish dark hair that gave the impression of being dyed or tinted. She had beady blue eyes and a sharp, thin nose, and even at a glance I noticed the wrinkles on her face and around her neck. She was wearing a loose dress, and although she might have had a good figure at one time, she looked dumpy now. There's not a nice way to say it. She looked like an old whore.

I heard the keys jingle again when she was past me, and then I heard her call out in a cheery voice.

"Oh, there you are, honey."

31

I heard Helen say something in what seemed like an apologetic tone, but I couldn't pick up the words. I stopped my horse so I could listen. Then I heard the older woman speak in a low, bossy voice. I didn't like the sound of it, so I turned my horse around and walked it back in the direction of the two women.

We had an awkward moment or two there. Helen seemed to be pretending not to notice me even though she was facing my way, and the old hag seemed to be twisting her shoulders to keep her back to me. That was a queer little game, I thought, so I spoke up.

"Say, Helen, are you sure you're all right?"

She gave a forced smile again as she said, "Oh, I'm fine."

"Well, I hope you'll excuse me if I'm not minding my own business, but for a minute there it looked as if you might not be free to come and go as you please."

Her face took on a simple look as she shook her head. "Oh, no. Everything is fine. This is my aunt." She smiled toward the old lady, who had taken her by the elbow and now turned my way.

"How do you do?" I said, touching my hat.

The old lady smiled like she had gas pains, and Helen said, "This is my aunt Maud. Auntie, this gentleman is . . . excuse me, I don't think you said your name when you passed by a few minutes ago. We hardly exchanged three words."

Of course I had told the girl my name, but I could tell she didn't want the older woman to know she had talked to me that much. "My name's Jimmy Clevis," I said, looking at Helen and then her chaperone.

The old lady didn't bat an eye, just tucked back the corners of her mouth to set off the wrinkles on her neck. I wondered if her neck turned red when she got mad, or if it always looked that way. It was reddish, like a rash, and what with that and the wrinkles, she looked a little bit like a turkey buzzard, but maybe not quite that far gone.

"Well, it's thoughtful of you to show concern," she said. Then, putting her right arm around Helen's shoulders, she added, "But I don't think there's any need for it here."

With that she put the girl into motion, and the two of them headed in the direction they had come from. There wasn't much for me to do but keep going in the opposite direction, so I did. But I sure

33

wasn't satisfied. I doubted that that old hag was any more Helen's aunt than she was mine, and I wondered what kind of a hold she had on the girl.

It gave me something to think about as I rode down the street and doubled back around. My idea was to look in back of the Jack-Deuce as well as in front before I went in. If I recognized a horse out of either Rudd's or Turner's string, I wouldn't go in. But the coast was clear, at least from the outside, so I tied up my horse in front.

I didn't like the feeling of skulking around, but it went away as I stepped into the Jack-Deuce. Sometimes it gives me a sense of freedom to be able to walk into a saloon in the middle of the day and not give a damn about anyone; and even if I didn't get the full feeling of it at that moment, I felt a hell of a lot better than I had at the boar's nest. And the whiskey smelled better, too. Even when I'm not going to drink whiskey, I like the familiar smell of it in a saloon.

I paused inside the door to let my eyes adjust. That's one drawback about going from full daylight into a place like the Jack-Deuce, but even that's not as bad as going back out into a glaring sun after having a few drinks and getting well relaxed. Going in, a fellow still has his wits about him and a little bounce. That's how I felt, and after looking into a dark corner to get my night eyes, I stepped toward the bar.

As I ordered a glass of beer and waited for it, I looked around to my left to see if there was anyone I would like to talk to. In the middle of the barroom, two tables away from the bar, sat a man named Tom. I raised my left hand in a wave, and he waved back. When my beer came, I picked it up and strolled over in the direction of Tom's table.

A lamp hung overhead between the first table and the second, so I could see Tom well enough. His thin, gray hair and matching Vandyke beard were neat as usual, and his eyeglasses were shining in the lamplight. I remember him telling me one time, with the attitude of a fellow who locked up his liquor cabinet in front of your very eyes, that men developed spectacles so the world would not be run by pups like me. A fellow could like Tom easy enough. He was a free spirit, and he made it clear he didn't have to try to please anybody. It worked both ways. He could tell me to my face that I was an upstart, and then he could make it clear to the rest of the world that if he wanted to be friends with the likes of me, he would, and he didn't care a fig for what anybody thought of it.

As I approached his table, he invited me to join him. I noticed a second drink glass, with about one finger of whiskey in it, at Tom's left. I wondered if he was expecting someone to come back, but he didn't give any indication. He picked up his pipe, which had been sitting on the table in front of him, and struck a match to light it. With the pipe in his teeth, and not looking at anything except the match flame that dipped down and then rose up, he said, "How's the weather?"

"Oh, fair enough, I guess."

"I heard it got pretty hot yesterday. Any of it come your way?"

I raised my eyebrows. "Not to me personally. But I guess you heard someone got to Jimmy Rooks."

The sound of clinking coins came from the bar. I turned around and saw the bartender sorting out a small heap of money on the bar top. I turned back to Tom and restated my question. "So you heard something?"

"That I did. The word came across from Mexican town. They said you found him but didn't have time to stick around, so I

36

thought you might be long gone."

I felt a sinking feeling. I had hoped Chanate wouldn't mention my name, but now I realized I should have been more particular and delivered the message myself. "I guess I didn't handle it very well," I said.

"No one seemed too bothered by it."

"By what? By Jimmy dying, or by my not staying around?"

"Either one, I guess."

"Did Chanate come over and report it, then?"

"Oh, yeah. Him and Kee-koe."

That was how Tom pronounced Quico. The Mexicans, they say things nice and sharp and clipped, but Tom's Spanish was like a knife that could never take or hold an edge. He knew a lot of it, but he just knocked the edges off half the words he said. Sometimes after I've heard him talk, I'll catch myself a day or two later mimicking the way he said something. For all that, they liked him in Mexican town, and that was part of the reason he and I were friends. We both got along well with the Mexicans. And we shared some attitudes about the world, whether he was here in the Jack-Deuce throwing his gibes at the big shots or dancing with the *solteronas* and *viudas* — the old maids and the widows — on the other side of the river. He was sort of homely, with a large head on a thin body so that he looked like a pumpkin on a fence post. But he was always clean and well-groomed, and he had good manners, especially with the old ladies, so you had the feeling that one of these days he would end up under the same roof with one of them. The Mexicans all treated him with respect, what with his gray hair and glasses, and they all called him Tome, so it rhymed with "home." When I thought of him, the word "Tome" ran through my mind, and that was how I began to refer to him to myself.

"So anyway, word got around."

Tome put his palm over the pipe and puffed out a cloud. "Oh, yeah."

"What seems to be the general opinion on why it happened?"

"Nothin' deep. All I've heard is that Jimmy probably got caught doing something."

"So you haven't heard anything more specific."

"No, just that. If there's a queer rooster somewhere, I haven't heard from him."

"What's that?"

"What?"

"You said some kind of a rooster."

"Oh, a queer rooster. That's a fellow that informs on others. It's like he pretends to sleep at night and then hears what the other chickens are up to."

"Sort of like a stool pigeon."

"Sort of, but a stool pigeon can work the other way around, and tell on honest people. Your queer rooster just tells on thieves and cutthroats and such."

"Oh." I took a drink of my beer. "So then, you haven't heard anything in particular."

"No. Should I have?"

"I don't know. I'm still in the dark as to why it happened, so that's why I'm asking you."

"Oh, then you weren't anywhere around."

"No, I just found him. I was supposed to meet him at the crossing, and someone had already dumped him there in the rocks."

"Hmph." Tome puffed on his pipe. "So they probably knew you were supposed to be there, and they counted on you finding him."

"I imagine it could have worked that way."

"And then you got in a hurry to go home

and milk the cows?"

"Not all that much. I did have to go back to the ranch, but the main thing was I didn't want to get all tied up answering questions with the sheriff."

Tome yawned. "Well, he hasn't gotten very worked up about it."

"In other words, he doesn't seem to care too much about who did it or why."

"Sort of seems that way."

"Well, I thought it was something that deserved looking into. Otherwise, I might not have taken so much trouble to get it reported."

"Hell, he'd just as well have been a Mexican, for as much as any of these sons of bitches care."

I got his meaning. No one cared about Jimmy Rooks because they assumed he was some kind of a shady character. Maybe he was, but in my eyes that didn't make him any less of a human. Call a man a rustler, or call him a Mexican, and you don't have to take it serious if something happens to him. I shook my head.

"There's Goings," said Tome.

"What's that?"

"I said, there's Goings." He dipped his head to the left.

"Oh." I looked up and saw a stranger

standing by the table, so I half rose in my seat and reached across to shake his hand. "I'm Jimmy Clevis."

"Pleased to meet you. My name's Goings. Al Goings."

As the man sat down by the almost-empty glass, I got a look at him. He had long hair, between light brown and dark blond, and a sparse beard of the same color. He had brown eyes with clear whites to them, and he looked alert even if he was a bit scraggly. He wore a slouch hat and loose-fitting clothes, and I wouldn't have been surprised to find out he wasn't the first owner of the shirt or pants. Although he wasn't dirty or grimy, he had an overall filmy appearance as if he got along well in places where water was in short supply.

I noticed that he touched his drink glass but did not raise it for a sip. There wasn't much whiskey left in it, so I imagined he was trying to make it last.

"What do you do?" he asked.

"Oh, I'm a ranch hand," I said, glancing at Tome, who seemed to ignore what I said. "And you?"

"I'm not doin' much of anything right now," he said. "I worked with the bone crews for a while, but that's just about done."

I nodded. I had seen fellows like him before, out on the prairie putting buffalo bones into heaps and then coming by with wagons to haul them to a rail station. One day I had watched them for an hour or so from up on a little hill, where I sat in the shade of my horse. I thought they looked forlorn, wandering around in the vast country and picking up dead things. "Yeah," I said, "there's not much of that left, unless you get a long ways from the railroads. What did you do before that?"

"I worked with the hide hunters."

The ones that left the bones, I thought. Another business that went bust. "Well, are you pretty handy around horses and other livestock, then?" I couldn't see him taking over Jimmy Rooks's job, but it made for conversation.

"No, not really. When I worked with the hide hunters I got kicked pretty bad one time, and now I've got something in here that won't let me get too close to horses or mules." He pointed at his temple.

"Sort of a fear, then."

He took a short, deep breath and let it out. "I guess you could call it that, but I don't feel scared. I just can't get close to 'em."

I took another drink of my beer. "Well,

that's too bad. Unless you want to go to work mining or wood-chopping, there's not much work out here where you aren't around animals. Oh, and shockin' wheat, if you stay over east a ways."

"That's what it seems like. There's work with freighters, and packers, and cow out-fits, and —"

"I told him he ought to get into a line of work he can find in bigger towns or cities," Tome said.

I hiked one leg over another and sat back in my chair. "Oh, yeah. Like in a ware-house."

Tome took a sip of his whiskey and held the glass in the air, halfway between his chin and the table. "I told him he could be a labor agitator."

I turned my head and looked at Goings. I didn't know if Tome was serious. "What do you think?"

"I told him I thought they usually brought in mounted policemen to break up those things, and there I'd be, running from horses again."

"That's a good point," I said. "But you know, I've knocked around in a lot of dif-ferent jobs, and I don't mean to be tellin' you anything, because you're probably a little older than I am —"

"No, that's fine. Go ahead."

"Well, if you know how to do kitchen work, at least there's always eats. And you get to a big town, and sometimes even a small one, and you can find work at it."

Goings nodded. "I've thought of it."

I wondered if he had some fear there, too, like of soapy water, but I didn't say anything. I took another look at the fellow, and I had a moment of sympathy. Here he was, down and out, probably not much over thirty, but hamstrung as far as what he could do. And here I was, a few years younger, but still full of bounce. I figured I could work at just about anything I wanted, except maybe a chimney sweep's apprentice, which I had heard scary stories about when I was small and kind of skinny myself. But I didn't have anything holding me back as far as normal jobs went, and talking with this fellow made me feel more fortunate.

Maybe that's what he wanted, because the next thing I knew, I'd bought him a drink. It looked as if Tome had bought him the first one but wasn't going to buy him a second, so I ordered a round for all of us. What little gloom there had been was lifted now, and everyone was cheery. This fellow Goings had a bit of wit to him, and Tome was telling him he could write pamphlets for labor agitators and anarchists to distribute.

"From the security of your own cottage," he said. "Far from the madding crowd."

Goings laughed. "The more I think about it, the more I like the idea of washing dishes and peeling spuds. I can work my way up from there."

The conversation hit a lull for a moment, and I thought of something I could ask Tome about. We hadn't mentioned Jimmy Rooks since Goings sat down, sort of by unspoken agreement, it seemed, but the other question came from right here in town.

"Say, Tome," I said, "do you know anything about a girl named Helen that lives in this town? Blond girl, maybe twenty or so."

Tome rubbed his palm down his chin beard. "Sure don't."

"She seems to be watched over by some old lady she calls her aunt. I thought there was something bogus about it."

"Oh? What's the aunt's name?" Tome seemed to perk up at the mention of the older woman.

"Maud."

"Oh. *Maud*," he said.

"You know her, then?"

He held up his hand. "Only from a distance."

"Well, what's the story on her?"

Tome raised his eyebrows and sniffed. "She and her, um, business associate run the boardinghouse right off Main Street. This girl Helen might be one of her girls. They come and go."

"What kind of a boardinghouse is it?" asked Goings.

"They actually have boarders, and a kitchen, but I don't think you'll find a job there. Her partner — name's Warlick, I think — does the cooking, and they've got a midget girl that does the dish-washing and cleaning."

"Huh," I said. "What about the other girls?"

"Oh, I think she keeps one or two of them for other purposes. It's just what I've heard. I don't know for sure."

"Funny I haven't heard about it."

"Oh, it's not a common kind of brothel or hog ranch. I think she sees it as being a little more elite. It probably runs more by invitation or personal reference."

I recalled the jingling keys. "So what kind of person is this woman Maud?"

"I haven't had an interview with her, but

from what I've seen, I'd say she's an old harlot who's seen her day."

That was one thing I liked about Tome. He didn't mince his words. "So," I said, "it doesn't sound like a fellow could just walk in and ask to see one of the girls."

"Probably not at all. I'd say that if you came in off the street, the only women you'd get to see would be old Maud and the midget."

Chapter Three

When I left the Jack-Deuce the sun was still high and bright, but I had drunk only two glasses of beer, so I didn't feel dizzy in the head or out of touch with my hands and feet. Even if I had been sitting around in a saloon at midday swapping small talk, I thought of myself as being on serious business. I had picked up a few scraps from Tome, but I wanted to see what else I might be able to learn before I went back to the range and the line camp.

As I led my horse across the street to the water trough and let him drink, I reminded myself that my main business was to find out whatever talk there was about how Jimmy Rooks came to grief. But the image of that girl kept crowding in. I would think of how nice she looked walking down the street, and then I would recall the simple, almost vacant expression on her face when the old strumpet got ahold of her. The girl had my curiosity up, and Tome's brief remarks about Maud and the midget girl made me even more interested in what was going on.

When my horse lifted his dripping muzzle up out of the trough, I led him away and mounted up. I put him into a walk down the middle of Main Street, then turned off to the left on the first side street. I rode up and down a couple of streets that way, looking for a place that might be a boardinghouse. I didn't expect to see the girl Helen, but I thought I might catch a glimpse of her keeper or of a short girl, and then I would know where the place was if I wanted to go by there again. I rode past the place where I met the girl, just to fix it in my mind. I assumed her lodging place was on another street, and after crossing Main Street two more times I rode past a place on my right that I thought might be it.

The building stood by itself, a two-story frame affair with an empty space on either side and some small outbuildings in back. It looked somewhat like a hotel, with a large single-pane window on each side of the doorway, which was set in from the sidewalk. I gave the place a full glance as I rode by. The windows looked in on a sitting room, which was vacant at this hour. I didn't see a registration desk or anything of that sort, such as you might find in a hotel, and there wasn't any sign hanging over the doorway or sticking out overhead above the sidewalk.

When I had ridden past, I decided to ride around the next block and then come back at the place from the other direction. About five minutes later, then, I was riding back toward Main Street with the place on my left. I tried not to look at it directly this time, so I was almost even with it when I saw a person standing in the doorway. Set back as it was, the entry was in shadow, but the door itself was open, so I could see the outline or form of the person.

It was a man, about average height with a heavy build. I could see dark hair and thick eyebrows set off against a light-colored face, at least the upper part. The lower part looked as if it needed a shave. The man stood in what looked like a rigid posture, but stoop-shouldered, and he held a broom resting upright at his side like a musket in an old illustration. I didn't think he had come out to do any sweeping. Rather, I thought he had the broom as part of a not-very-good disguise, of an idle shopkeeper or businessman come out to watch the traffic. If that was his intent, it didn't work. He looked like what I took him to be — Maud's business associate, as Tome had put it. Or, to use a word I had heard in my early years, I think in church, he fit my notion of a procurer. He looked jealous enough for the role, guarding the doorway and watching me as I rode by. He barely moved, but he did turn, as I could tell from the ripple of a watch chain. Then he was gone from even the corner of my vision, and I could feel his eyes still on me. I thought either he or Maud had seen me the first time I rode by.

Well enough. I was done with them for the time being. I rode on to Main Street, turned left, and then went south until I came to the plank bridge. I crossed it, *thumpity-thump*, and rode into Mexican town.

The first thing I needed to do was to go see Chanate, so I headed for his butcher shop. There weren't very many people out and about at this time of the day, so I rode along unbothered, thinking of how I might phrase things once I got into the conversation with Chanate. I can bring out my ideas well enough in Spanish, but sometimes I run through the wording of this little thing or that so I won't be cold when I start talking. I realized I might have put Chanate on the spot by the way I did things the day before, and I needed to clear that up. So I had a few words and phrases singing through my mind, and within a couple of minutes I was enjoying the sounds as much as the meanings.

Some of the words are musical — Chanate's name, for example. It's got three syllables, and you hit the middle one so it rhymes with *to-MA-te*. It's like the way they say coyote, *co-YO-te*, so much prettier than "caw-oat," like a lot of the punchers pronounce it. Then *guajolote*, the turkey, and *zopilote*, the buzzard, and *tecolote*, the owl. Musical words, if you hear them the way the Mexicans say them, with the edges still on them. Same with *Chanate*, *tomate*, and *chocolate*. As for his name, it means blackbird, or what some people call grackle or starling, the kind of bird that comes and goes in a flock. They've got a million nick-names, these people. I knew a fellow they called Cuervo, the crow, and another they called Tlacuache, the opossum. For all I know, either of them, or my friend Chanate, could have been christened Arnulfo.

Soon enough I came to the butcher shop, where I tied my horse at the hitching rail and went inside. A bell tinkled as I closed the door behind me. It was dark and cool in the shop, rich with the smell of suet and garlic and fresh meat. As my eyes adjusted I could see hams and sides of bacon hanging on the wall in back of the counter, and chains of sausages hanging at either end. I caught movement at the blanket that separated the shop from the living quarters in back, and then I saw my friend Chanate, small and dark-featured, smiling as he recognized Yimi. We shook hands and spoke in Spanish, as always.

"Hello, Yimi. How does it go?"

"More or less."

"Well, I'm happy to see you."

"The same here. And how is Tina?"

"Fine, fine. And you? Is everything all right at the ranch?"

"Well, nothing happened to me. But of course, my friend —"

"Poor fellow. It hurt us that your friend should die."

"Me too. I don't know why they did it."

"Oh, so you weren't there."

"No, I found him. I think I told Carlos that."

"Probably so."

"Yes, I found him like that, with a bullet. I'm sorry I didn't have time to come and tell you in person."

"That's all right."

"Afterwards, I thought I should have. But at that moment, I wanted to stay away.

You know, from the sheriff and all that. So I thought I could send a message. Then I thought I put too much on you."

"Don't worry about it. No one gave me any trouble."

"I knew I could count on you, but I should have come in person."

"But you were in a hurry."

"Yes, but I could have done that much." I thought about saying that I could have given him an idea of what to say or not say, and then I realized it might have seemed presumptuous to want to work out a story and then make someone else tell it. Along the same line, I thought it might seem rude now to tell him I could have done it then.

"Well, you came now. So everything's fine. I thought you would come."

"I knew I had to come, to tell you myself how it happened, and to ask, also, if you have heard any gossip."

"You mean about the death?"

"Yes."

He shook his head. "Nothing, really. Just that he probably did something, and that's what happens." Chanate looked at me as if he was sorry to say anything that might be taken as personal.

"Who knows?" I said. "That's what Tome said he heard."

"Oh, yes. Tome knows a great deal."

"It doesn't seem to me that anyone knows very much. Maybe my friend did something, but it didn't look like he got killed that way."

Chanate raised his eyebrows. "I don't think they killed him for no reason."

"Well, what I mean is, I don't think they did it because he took something that wasn't his. They would do it in a different way. I think it was for something else."

"What could it be?"

I shrugged. "I don't know. That's why I wish I could hear something."

"It's barely one day. Maybe something will come up."

"Maybe."

"And the other companions?"

I assumed his use of the word *compañeros* referred to Rudd and Turner. "What about them?"

"What do they say?"

"The same. They say someone must have caught him doing something."

"You don't think they know who did it?"

"I don't think they want to know anything."

"Who knows?" said Chanate. "They're the closest. Maybe they know something they don't tell you." He gave me a confidential nod. "Watch out for yourself, Yimi."

"I know."

"Until you know why they did this to your friend, you don't know if they want to come after you. They're sons of bitches."

"Oh, I know. They're sons of bitches, for sure." I liked being able to talk with such certainty when we didn't have an idea of who it was we were talking about.

"But it would be very good to know why they did it."

"Oh, yes."

"Do you think he could have done something without realizing it?"

I liked the way he rolled out the last phrase, *"sin darse cuenta,"* clipped and clear. It was one of those phrases that Tome flattened out: "seen darsy cuentuh." I pondered the question as I appreciated the phrase itself.

Chanate spoke again. "You know, sometimes a person does something without knowing what it means to someone else. And the thing he does, he doesn't pay it any attention. Then it brings him consequences."

I turned it over for a second. "It might have been something like that. Maybe he got into something that was deeper than he thought."

Chanate shrugged. "An idea, nothing more. Who knows?"

"That's true." I glanced around the shop, wondering what other topic I might bring up.

Chanate spoke. "And how is Tome? What does he say?"

I recalled the scene at the Jack-Deuce. "Oh, he's fine. I talked with him for a little while."

"He is very good, Tome. He knows many things."

"Yes, he knows a lot." I had a fleeting memory of a girl walking down the street. "Sometimes I wish he knew more."

"Well, yes."

"About this thing, yes, and about others."

"Oh, yes."

I felt that he was inviting me to go ahead, so I said, "I saw something that seemed strange to me."

"Really?"

"Yes, it was over there, in town. It was a girl and her aunt. At least she said it was her aunt. I asked Tome about it, and he said the aunt has a place where people stay or eat meals but it isn't a hotel."

"Oh, a guest house. A lodging place."

"That's it. He told me the woman and

her companion have the business."

"Oh, I don't know."

"Maybe you've seen the people. You go over there sometimes."

"More often they come here, like you and Tome. But, yes, I go there."

"Well, the girl is young and blond and pretty." With my two hands I made out the curved figure of a woman.

Chanate smiled. "Sometimes I see one like that. Maybe I should go look now."

"She's about twenty years old, has blue eyes, and her name is Helen."

He shook his head. "I don't think I know her."

"Well, all right. The older woman has brown hair, almost red, and a very white face. She looks like she used to be a woman of the street."

Chanate raised his eyebrows. "I'm not sure."

"And her companion has dark hair and he's a little —" I stooped over and made a curving motion with my hand over my shoulder.

"*O, sí, medio jorobado.*"

I had to pick that one apart. I thought I remembered *jorobado* meant hunchback, so I stooped over even more and made the curving motion in the air in front of me.

When Chanate smiled and nodded, I knew he meant the fellow was half hunchback.

"Do you know him, then?"

"I know who he is. And I think I have seen the woman."

"The witch and the hunchback."

Chanate laughed. "Yes, but he isn't a real hunchback. You know, a hunchback is good luck. Some people say so. You rub the hump, and it gives you good luck. If he is authentic."

"This one doesn't look like that."

"No, I don't think so. Just half, no more."

"So, do you know anything about their business?"

"No, I don't know the place. I've just seen him on the street, and I think I've seen the old woman with him."

"And the girl?"

He shrugged. "I've seen some two or three, maybe, on the street in the daytime, but I don't distinguish them."

"It doesn't matter much."

I began to wonder what time it was. We had been standing there talking for several minutes, and no one had come into the shop. I knew that things slowed down in the *colonia* from one till three, and it occurred to me that I might have interrupted

Chanate's *siesta* or maybe even his meal.

"Do you know what time it is?" I asked.

"It's going to be three. Did you eat already?"

"No, I didn't."

"You didn't eat with Tome?"

"No, I think he already ate."

He held up a finger and said, "Just a moment." Then he went to the blanket and called into the living quarters, announcing that here was Yimi and he had not eaten. Then, as he looked back at me, he put his thumb and fingertips together and pointed them at his mouth, to mean food, and he winked.

I nodded and smiled.

I had been in their house a few times before, so it was a comfortable feeling to go through the storeroom, the living room, and on into the kitchen and eating area. The smell of hot grease and fried corn tortillas hung in the air, and I felt happy as I took off my hat.

Chanate's wife, Clementina, turned from the stove and came to meet me. She was a short, happy person, with a nice rounded figure, not as slender as her husband and not as dark. She had a tan complexion, shoulder-length black hair, and eyes like dark coffee. She smiled as always as she gave me her hand and told me to sit down.

I took a seat at the wooden table and looked up to see the plaster-of-Paris plaque of the Last Supper that hung on the wall. Someone had painted it long ago in bright colors, mainly blues and reds and purples. Most of the Mexican houses I've been in have been civilized that way, with crucifixes and saints' figurines and pictures of Christ, and sometimes pictures of the Virgin of Guadalupe and Mary Madeline, I think she's called. It always gives me a decent feeling to sit down in a house like that and not have to feel the weight of it all. I've broken bread, much earlier in life, with staunch Methodists and Baptists, and I always felt guilty for not letting them convert me. I didn't feel that way in a Mexican household. For one thing, they never begrudge anyone a meal. It's free, from the goodness of God, as they see it, and it doesn't come with a price of guilt or a sense of debt. People like Chanate and Tina would open up their house to the likes of me, let me know it was always my house, and still let me be the heathen I was.

Chanate said he had to go out to the store, so he left me to sit by myself at the table. I was used to that, so I sat and looked at the Last Supper as Tina heated food and threw out an occasional question about work and the weather. Then she brought me a plate with a heap of mashed beans and a serving of fried chunks of pork. Next to that she set a stack of corn tortillas wrapped in a towel, and she went back to the kitchen.

I went to work on the food, using pieces of tortilla to pick it up. At one point she asked me if I would like some coffee, but she caught me with a mouthful of food, so I wagged my pointer finger back and forth to say no. She waited and asked if I would like some water, and when my mouth was clear I said yes.

Talk was limited with Tina, because she knew I didn't have a family to ask about. For some reason she and Chanate didn't have children, so the house wasn't full of children or grandchildren. I knew some of their nieces and nephews, like Nena, who lived in the *colonia,* and Quico, who worked at a sheep camp. Sometimes Tina had a comment about one of them, but not much. She didn't ask me very much about my work or where I lived, maybe because she didn't care to ask personal questions and maybe because she already knew enough. And if she knew anything about what had happened to my *compañero,* I'm sure she would have considered it something she didn't talk about. And I wouldn't have been surprised to know that the news about the dead man had not made it this far into the house.

I ate a second helping of food, half as big as the first, and finished the stack of tortillas. I thanked Tina for the food, and she thanked God, so I did, too. Then, at her suggestion, I went back out front to visit some more with Chanate.

He had a lamb carcass hung up on a pair of meat hooks and was sawing it in half, right down the backbone. I stood and watched as he held one haunch steady with his left hand and sawed with his right. He stood facing the spine, so the nose of the saw moved back and forth through the cavity of the animal. I enjoyed watching him do a nice, neat job of it until he had the carcass hanging in two halves.

He was in the process of cutting the left shoulder away from the ribs when the bell on the front door tinkled. A gray-haired woman all in black came in, said *"Buenas tardes,"* and began to tell Chanate what she wanted. It sounded as if he was going to be busy cutting up a couple of chickens, so I took the opportunity to say good-bye. We shook hands, he wished me well, I nodded good-bye to the *viuda* as I put on my hat, and I was out the door with the bell tinkling behind me.

I looked at the sky and saw that the sun was off to the west. I didn't have much time to waste, but there was one more place I wanted to drop in on before I headed back. I rode out to the main street, turned left toward the bridge, went two blocks, and turned right. I went east until I came to the middle of the third block, where a little stuccoed house sat back from the street about twenty yards. I hoped Magdalena was home.

Nena, as she was called, was Chanate and Clementina's niece. Usually an unmarried girl her age would still live with her parents, but from what I understood, they lived down in Colorado Springs, and she didn't see eye-to-eye with them. She had some sort of truce with Chanate and Tina, who didn't criticize how she lived as long as she kept it to herself.

Magdalena was the kind of girl I got along with really well. She didn't judge my life, and I didn't judge hers. We had both been knocked around enough that we often saw things the same way, which is to say not very rosy; but she was still a woman, and a

64

fine-looking one at that, and I treated her like one. She appreciated it and would sometimes say I was *muy caballero,* a real gentleman. I couldn't be any other way with a polite, attractive girl like her, and besides, she always made me feel excited to be around her, as if maybe someday we would get further in our friendship.

I knocked on the door a couple of times, and finally she opened it a crack and then pulled it open all the way.

"Yimi," she said. "What a surprise." Actually, in Spanish they say "What a miracle," but it means surprise.

"Good afternoon, Nena. I came by here to say hello to you."

"Oh, how nice. Come in." She stood aside to let me in.

I took off my hat and made my way to a wooden chair I had sat in before.

"Can I give you something? Have you eaten?"

"Yes, I just ate with your aunt."

"Oh, good. Something else?"

"Um, no thanks. I just came to talk."

"Very well."

She took a seat in the one stuffed chair in the room. I got a nice look at her, as the curtain was drawn on the east side of the room and the daylight came in. Her long, dark hair, which she sometimes kept tied back, hung loose over her shoulders. She had put on red lipstick, and it made a lovely contrast with her tan complexion. She was wearing a plain, dark cotton dress, but everything about her was sending off sparks. At least that's how it felt to me.

I started out in a deliberate way. "I imagine you have heard that a partner of mine had some bad luck."

She nodded. "Yes, I heard he passed away. I am sorry."

"Well, I don't know why it happened. Everyone says he probably got found out for something, but I don't think it was other ranchers or anything like that. But I don't know what else it could be."

She shrugged. "I don't know, Yimi. I haven't heard anything, just that he got killed."

"Did you know him?"

She shook her head. "No."

"Well, if you hear something, I would appreciate it if you told me."

"Of course."

"So that's it. A big thing, but very little to say about it." I rotated my hat where it sat on my knee, and then I looked straight at her again. "I have another question."

"Go ahead."

"This is something else, but it caught my attention. There's a girl over there in town, and I think they have her closed up in a hotel. Well, no, not a hotel. A guest house."

She gave me a serious look, and I noticed her green eyes for the first time that day. "Do you think they have her sequestered, against her will?"

"I don't know. But it seems strange to me."

"Which place is it?"

"It's a guest house, on a street on the right side of the central street."

"Do you know the owner?"

"I think there are two people. An old witch and a hunchback."

She laughed. "I think I know the place. They have an *enanita* that works there."

"What's that?"

"An *enanita?* A very short girl."

"Oh, yes. Tome told me about her, but I didn't see her. I saw the others, the witch and the hunchback."

She smiled again at my language and then asked, "Does the girl work there?"

"I don't know. Tome says it's a guest house, but it might be the other kind as well."

"Tome knows many things."

I smiled. "Does that mean you think it's

the other kind of house, too?"

She shrugged, lighter this time. "Tome knows better than I do. He is from there, and he is older."

"Well, I just met the girl, so I don't know much about her. But if they're keeping her shut up, that's not all right."

"Do you like her, Yimi?"

"Oh, I don't know. She got my attention."

"Does she like you?"

I shook my head. "I don't think she knows me well enough."

"If she likes you, you have to do something. And if she doesn't, don't get yourself into any trouble."

"I would just like to see her again, to know more."

"Of course."

"I'm curious, that's all."

"Of course, but if she doesn't like you, she's not worth the trouble. Find yourself another girl. What does she look like, Yimi? Is she pretty?"

"Yes, she's pretty. She's a blonde." I felt like saying "blondie girl" in English, the way I had heard a dark-haired girl say it one time, but I didn't.

"That's nice. Blondes are pretty."

I felt she was making it too easy for me. "Some of them," I said. I hesitated and then went on. "If you hear anything about her, will you tell me?"

"Of course, Yimi. And if it looks like trouble, I'll tell you that, too."

"Oh, yes. I trust you, Nena."

"That's good. You have a good heart, Yimi."

"Thank you." I knew that was as far as I was going to get in the conversation, so without any ceremony I stood up. "I have to go. I'm sorry to be in a hurry." I wanted to move close to her as she stood up, but I kept my distance and said, "You're the best, Nena."

"Thank you, Yimi. I hope you find your girl."

I hoped so, too. But all the way back to the line camp I wanted to kick myself in the ass. Why didn't I just make a play for Nena? I asked myself. And the answer was that I was afraid. I knew she had other men. I wasn't afraid of it in just the factual sense, because for all I knew, this girl Helen was the same or worse. What I was afraid of was that I wouldn't be able to get a girl like Magdalena to choose me above the others. Or, to draw it finer, I was afraid to try. So instead, I was asking her to help me find a blondie girl. If anyone ever deserved a kick in the ass, it was me.

Chapter Four

Nobody had much to say that evening when I got back to the line camp. Rudd was sitting on the doorstep in the shade of the building, paying close attention to a pair of hobbles he was mending, and Turner was sitting on a crate not far away. He had his jackknife out and was scraping the deep smears of dirt on the upper part of his pants leg. He asked if I had seen anything, which always had at least two meanings, and I said no, nothing in particular. I put my horse away and loitered by the pasture gate for a little while, then went to see if the other two fellows had any more to say. They had gone inside, so I went in to join them.

The air was stifling inside the boar's nest, but that didn't stop Rudd from rolling a cigarette and lighting it. Turner was chunking firewood into the woodstove, so I could see the air wasn't going to thin out much. I went to work rustling up the same kind of grub we'd had the night before, and I wondered whether this kind of life, just going from one day to the next, ever got stale for the other two.

As I was cutting slices of salt pork, I remembered that we were supposed to take a ride the next day up into the foothills to the west. "I wonder if we might find some other kind of meat tomorrow," I said. "Give us a little variety."

Rudd blew out a stream of cigarette smoke and said, "No tellin'."

Turner closed the door of the stove and stood up. "That should give us plenty to cook on," he said.

I didn't like being shut out of conversation like that, so I said, "I'd go for some deer meat if we came across some."

"I'm not that stuck on it myself," Turner answered. "The last one we had was so tough, I had a hard time gittin' it down."

Rudd laughed. "Gives him bad dreams. Makes him think the dark brother has him by the throat again."

It came back to me, Turner's story about why he couldn't eat fast and why sometimes he had a hard time swallowing. As he told it, a "big black bastard" had choked him almost to death one time, and his throat was never the same after that. Now that I thought of it, I wondered how much the world might have lost if the dark brother had done a better job. But that was the way life went. Jimmy Rooks was going

71

to have dirt thrown in his face in the next day or two, and Turner lived to complain about good food.

"By the way," I said. "Does anyone know when Jimmy's going to be buried?"

"Depends on what arrangements they make for him back home," Rudd said, in a matter-of-fact tone.

"Oh, really?" I looked at Turner, who said nothing.

Rudd spoke again. "Yeah. I went into town and told them to ship it to a town called Carthage, there in Missouri."

"Was that where he was from?"

"Either that or pretty close. I'd heard him mention it."

I tried to pick my words carefully. "What led you to do it that way?"

"The boss wanted to get him the hell away from here."

"Oh. You talked to the boss, then?"

"Sure. You don't let something like this just go past you."

"Uh-huh." It figured that he went to go see the boss and then had to talk to the sheriff. "When did you go to town, then?"

"About the time you were in the Jack-Deuce."

"Oh." That almost set me back, but I didn't let it. "Then I don't imagine we'll be going to Jimmy's funeral."

"Doesn't look like it."

Things were pretty quiet for the rest of the evening, and I felt that I was being kept on the outside of whatever was going on. I couldn't help wonder if it meant anything for me, like being told to pack my bag and bedroll. When we turned in for the night, I lay awake in my bunk for quite a while. Before too long, Rudd was snoring like a bulldog and Turner was taking deep, noisy breaths. I wondered if they slept too easy or if I made it too hard on myself. I tried thinking about one thing and another, and the impression that did me the best and finally helped me go to sleep was the picture I had of Magdalena, with her long, dark hair hanging over her shoulders.

The morning started out like any other, with a little rooting around in the boar's nest and then getting breakfast under way. Before long the smell of coffee and fried food hung on the air, and the day didn't seem too bad. Rudd and Turner were acting as if nothing had ever happened to cause a difference between us, but I was getting used to it. If they wanted to pretend that a problem was going to go away, I figured that was their choice. So I dug into my fried spuds and tried to be cheerful.

"We can get a fairly early start today," I said.

After a moment of silence, Rudd spoke without looking up. "We're not goin'."

"Oh," I said. "Did things get changed?" It had happened before, and now that I thought of it, this was the way it went. The boss would send orders for us to do something, and then at about the time we were getting ready to do it, we'd find out there was a change in plans. I usually didn't care, as it all paid the same, but this time it irked me. I saw it as a continuation of how I'd been dealt with the night before, and I realized that Rudd had gone out of his way not to tell me a simple little thing like this. If he had seen the boss at, say, noon or earlier on the day before, then he had known about the change in plans all the time.

Turner was keeping quiet, so I imagined it wasn't news to him.

Finally Rudd answered. "Yeah. Orders from the boss."

"Uh-huh. Is there a new plan, or do we just go out and do what we usually do?"

"Um, no. We're supposed to stick around here. The boss is goin' to come by."

"Must be somethin' important, if he's takin' the trouble to come all the way over here."

Rudd still didn't look up. "I didn't ask him," he said.

I nodded to myself. Rudd was a smart dodger, the way he phrased things. It was a good bet he knew why the boss was coming, and just as good a bet that I wouldn't find out till Whitlow got there. I let it pass, thinking that at least I knew the boss was on his way. And that wasn't all bad. I had seen very little of him in the year or so that I had worked for this outfit, and now I would get to take another look at him.

In the kind of work I did, a fellow didn't ask many questions about how things were managed. I knew that the boss was named Whitlow, that he had three or four line camps in addition to his headquarters, and that he called the whole outfit the Kite. But I didn't know how things were done at the other places, what kind of a setup Whitlow had at his own place, or even why he called it the Kite.

I think Rudd wanted us to look industrious, so he put us to work oiling the saddles and bridles and odds and ends of harness that hung in the lean-to. I didn't mind the work, but I wondered at the point of some of it, as most of the harness was stiff and wrinkled, and I had never

75

seen a wagon at this line camp. Turner and I worked away at it all, in no great hurry. I kept an eye out toward the west, figuring the boss would come from that direction, but he surprised me at about ten-thirty when he came riding in from the northeast.

He showed up alone, which reminded me of my general sense of him as a man that kept to himself. He didn't keep someone hanging around for protection, and as far as I knew, he didn't have any friends who spent much time with him, either. On this day he came riding in on a large sorrel horse with no markings, and even though the day was warming up, he wore a frock coat. I couldn't recall ever seeing him without one. All in all he was a clean fellow, maybe the type that was even a little prissy about getting his hands dirty. He had a good head of brown hair, which he kept neat, and he was always clean-shaven. As he got down from his horse, I noticed he was starting to get thick in the upper body. Being above average height, and filling out, he carried himself like the boss he was. He had a hard brow and a pair of dark blue eyes, and he seemed to have gotten good at glaring, just as he seemed to have learned to loom over others. For a man in his early or middle thirties, he was pretty sure of himself.

Rudd walked up to Whitlow and said a few words in a low voice. Then he called to Turner, told him to take care of the boss's horse, and led the way into the shack. Whitlow went in behind him.

I had been standing off to the side, ready to be called on if someone wanted to talk to me. Now I went back to my work. I could imagine Rudd telling the boss I had gone into town the day before, and it gave me a queasy feeling. I decided I wasn't going to tell any of them that I had been asking around about Jimmy Rooks. From the way I was being shut out of everyone else's conversation, I thought there was no reason to tell everything I knew or had done.

At about the time Turner finished putting the horse away, Rudd came to the doorway and told the two of us to come inside. I went in last, and right away the place felt crowded to me. I think it had something to do with coming in from a fresh, wide-open morning, but I think it had plenty to do with the presence of one more person as well. Whitlow sat at the table with his hat off and his coat open. I caught a glimpse of some kind of a watch chain, and then I ended up sitting across the corner of the table from him and didn't see as much. When he started in on us, I forgot about some of the smaller details.

"We can't be having this kind of trouble," he said, moving his hard gaze from Turner to me.

I gave a short nod.

Now he looked straight at me. "I'd like to know what you and Jimmy did to get him killed."

"I didn't do anything, not with him or without him."

"Well, he didn't get killed for nothing."

"I have no idea. He may have done something on his own. But I've got no way of knowing."

"That could be. I'm halfway convinced it could go on under your nose and you wouldn't know it."

I shrugged. "Could be."

"But I don't think Jimmy was that deep," he went on. "I think the two of you did something stupid."

"I don't know what it could be. We haven't lifted anything since that last little bunch we put together in July, and that went off slicker 'n hell."

Whitlow bored into me with those dark blue eyes. "Well, someone did something, that's for sure. It's caused some trouble, and I don't like it. You need to get this through your head: We don't want attention."

"Okay. I've got it."

"And when something happens, you keep your mouth shut."

"I know."

"Then what the hell did you go spill the beans for?"

"I don't know. There was something in the way he was killed — shot and then dumped off in the place where he was supposed to meet me. To my knowledge, if you get a few cattlemen together to take care of someone, they don't do things that way. They leave him hangin' in plain view somewhere, or they have someone put a bullet through him and leave him where he fell."

"To your knowledge." Whitlow's face drew tight. "For as much as you know, you're awfully damn lucky it hasn't happened to you. But even at that, why did you go tell someone?"

"Well, I guess it seemed like a normal killing — that is, the kind of thing that would happen to anyone. Or let me put it this way: It seemed like something that happened outside of anything we did, so I thought I should treat it as if it happened to someone else."

He narrowed his gaze at me again. "Just that simple, huh?"

"I wouldn't say it was simple, but I thought Jimmy deserved something."

"Oh, I see. On one hand, it was just as if it was no one in particular, and on the other hand, you did it because he was your friend."

"I thought —"

"You didn't think." He pointed at me with all four fingers, using his hand like a fin or a blade. "If you're going to think at all, remember what I tell you. We don't need attention."

"I understand."

"I don't know if you do. So I'll tell you plain. When you work with an outfit like this, you don't cross it."

"I don't believe I did that."

He gave me a cold stare. "You went outside the group. Do you understand that?"

I could see he was careful not to say anything like the word "gang," but his meaning was clear. "Yes," I said.

He shook his head. "You don't do that. Not with this outfit."

"I understand."

★ ★ ★

That afternoon, after Whitlow had ridden away, I saddled up and went out on a ride myself. I didn't like the way things were shaping up, and for all I knew, Whitlow was off behind a little knoll or bluff somewhere, watching me with a spyglass. I didn't care at the moment. I decided I would just go down to the river and watch it flow by. I didn't owe these sons of bitches anything, and I didn't like being made to feel that everything was my fault. So to hell with them, I thought. If I want to go down and watch the river flow, I will. That's not crossing anybody.

So I went down to a place that was a little more out of the way than the place where I had found Jimmy. I sat in the shade of a cottonwood tree and held on to my horse's reins as I gazed at the river. I could remember other times when I had sat like that and life was simple as pie. And it hadn't been that far back.

Even when I worked with the tie hacks, and I lived in a crowded camp full of coarse men, life was wide open. You worked, you slept, you ate, you drank. You stayed out of the way of swinging, razor-sharp axes just as you learned which men to stay away from. I remembered how, in the springtime, we all went down to the river to float the timbers downstream. There was a swarm of men, ranging from the ones that cut down the trees, to those that trimmed the logs into railroad ties and mine-shaft props, to mule skinners, to roughnecks that handled the chains and skids. It was a huge affair, with teams of men throwing timbers into the river, and then one day a big jam built up. The pieces started backing up and then piling up like sticks, and everyone was shouting orders, and half a dozen fellows with more guts than I've got went out dancing on the floaters and tried to break the jam loose with pikepoles. Then finally someone who knew how to do it blew up the jam with dynamite, and the whole damn mess started flowing down the river. Life went back to normal, just working and eating, drinking and sleeping, staying clear of the fights and thinking about the next time you might get close to a woman.

I had gotten out of that line of work because it was too boisterous. Things came to a high boil too often. But now as I looked back, I thought that at least I wasn't closed in like I was now.

I thought of all those logs on the river, and how some men had a knack for making hay while the sun was shining. They took what they could get, when they could get it. Most of the common workers would get payday drunk and end up broke, but a few of them, especially the ones higher up, came out of that business sittin' pretty good. And even if they made their money off of the efforts of other men, what they made was clean.

Then I remembered something a little farther back, when I was out in California knocking around. I met a fellow who told me how he made a pot of money killing ducks. He knew spots along the river where ducks would come in and land by the hundreds, and he would set up a whole line of shotguns with strings on the triggers. He would pick the right moment to jump the whole flock, and as the ducks lifted off the river he would set off a volley that would knock down fifty or a hundred of them. Then he would go out in a skiff and pick them up, and chase down any that were winged but not dead yet. After that he would haul the whole mess of dead ducks to a Chinaman in Sacramento. This duck hunter bought drinks for me a couple of times when he had just sold his catch, and I remember thinking that even if it seemed a little grabby to make money that way, it wasn't full of complications and it didn't take anything from anybody.

As I sat there watching the river and thinking about earlier days, other patches of memory came in. I thought about what it had been like, just a few years earlier, before I fell in with the kind of company I was keeping now. After drifting around here and there and trying my hand at one kind of work or another, I decided I liked ranch work as well as anything. So I ended up learning the cowpuncher trade in more detail. I guess I was a good cowboy, minding out for the outfit I rode for, never having to look over my shoulder for something I had done, and never having to worry if someone might be on the lookout for me and what I might do. Because at that time, I never lifted a thing.

But it was in me, like some kind of bug in my blood. Working with the freighters and the packers, the tie hacks and the miners, the ditch crews and the farm crews, I met all types. Of those that weren't straight as an arrow, some were low and crude enough that I could ignore them. But others were clever, sometimes educated and intelligent. They had an outlook that made everything look like a game or a good joke, and taking advantage of others was part of the play. I don't know if that way of life, with the fellows I met, put the bug in my blood or if it had been there all along and they woke it up little by little. I don't know, but a phrase like "the difference between right and wrong" wasn't any more than words to me. If anything, stealing was an equalizer, as it took away the distance between someone who had the money to pay for something and another fellow who wanted it and knew how to take it.

They say there are some diseases you can carry around for quite a while before they finally come out, and regardless of how I picked it up, that seems to be the way it happened to me. I was a good cowboy for a couple of years, working the season from spring to fall and then holing up in a comfortable place in the winter. After the second season, I got an offer from a couple of respectable cattlemen to brand mavericks for three dollars a head. That was good winter's work. I could make wages every month and still have time, when the weather was bad, to try out the comforts of town. Well, it wasn't a big step from there to working for a crooked outfit, then meeting someone who said he knew a better place, and so forth, until I found myself working for the Kite and living in a place that wasn't much better than a robbers' roost.

I could see it all as I sat by the river. I had been happy and carefree, but ripe as a peach that was ready to fall. There was a trick I learned in California, an honest one, that I didn't get to use very much in cow country but that I thought of from time to time. When the peaches started getting ripe, the first ones and some of the best ones were high up in the tree and on the outside, where they got the most sunlight. If a fellow wanted one of those better peaches, he could take a prop board out from under a branch and use it to reach up. He could put the notch of the board under the round, plump, fuzzy bottom of the peach, then nudge the board upward until the peach came loose. With a little luck, it rolled right down the board into his hands. Even though I didn't fall straight into one set of hands, I was ripe enough to be nudged. I could see it now. I had thought I was smart, doing something bold and getting away with it, living off my wits. But I was just a thief.

I had to think hard and go way back to recall a time when I wasn't a thief or wasn't thinking it was clever for someone else to be one. I had to go all the way back to the farm, when I had a father and a mother and a sister. My father drank, and he slapped around my mother and me, and I think he might have done things to my sister, but I didn't live among thieves. Life consisted of drudgery like sorting beans and plucking chickens, with better moments of wandering through the countryside and learning things in school in the presence of girls. It was so long ago it seemed like another life, and in a way it was, like a closed book. My mother died of appendicitis, and my sister ran off and came to a bad end, as I heard. Not too long after I left home, my father went off with a stroke, and that was the end of my connections with that earlier life.

I took a deep breath and hauled myself back to the present, where I sat a mile downstream from Red Wind Crossing, more or less hiding from my fellow thieves. It wasn't a good feeling, but at least I didn't have my head in a bucket. I knew I was in deep with this way of life, and I knew how I could end up if I didn't get out. I remembered talking with Jimmy Rooks about that very thing. It was easy talk, just wondering out loud whether a fellow might want to give it up someday and try something else. Now I knew I wanted out. But I also knew I was going to have to be damn careful and pick the time, because trying to get out of this outfit would probably fall in the category of crossing it.

Chapter Five

After I had sat by the river for quite a while and had sorted things out one way and another, I decided to go to town again. I didn't feel like going back to the line camp any sooner than I had to, and no one had said anything about not going to town. My main impression of what I could or couldn't do was that I was supposed to keep my mouth shut and not do anything that would cross the outfit.

My uppermost thought in going to town was to see if I could get a look at that girl again. I still had a good image of what she looked like walking down the street, and I thought I would like to follow up on that interest. I thought I might get to talk to her, and at the very least it would help me get my mind off the whole problem of what happened to Jimmy Rooks and what I might have to do to ease away from the Kite.

The sun had crossed its high point for the day when I turned into the street where I remembered finding the boarding-house. I didn't expect to see the girl right off, but I thought I could look things over and get a better idea of the layout of the place. Then, if I went there at different times, sooner or later I might get a chance to talk to her.

The entrance to the boardinghouse sat halfway down the block on the right side, and when I was about halfway there from the corner, I saw the figure of a person moving in and out of the entryway. It looked as if the person was sweeping, but I couldn't tell for sure, as the front of the building lay in shadow and the person was not very tall. At first I thought it was a kid, and then I remembered that the establishment had a hired girl who was, as Nena had put it, very short.

I stopped my horse. I thought it might be a good idea to approach the situation on foot, in case I got a chance to talk to the hired girl. So I turned the horse around, went back onto the main street, and tied him up. Then I walked down the sidewalk toward the boardinghouse. The person with the broom had worked her way out onto the sidewalk, and she had her back to me.

It was a short girl, all right. I could tell that much from the long skirt. I remembered Tome calling her a midget, and my general notion of that word was that it described a person who was short and thick, with stubby arms and legs and a broad face. This person just looked small, and I wondered if it would be more proper to call her a dwarf. I didn't know. I thought and thought, trying to hear Magdalena's voice, and then the word came to me light and clear: *enanita*.

I didn't want to walk up on her unexpectedly, so I clomped along the board sidewalk with my spurs jingling. When I was within about ten yards of her she turned around, and I got my first real look at the *enanita*.

She had tight, curly blond hair, split down the middle and hacked on both sides so that it just covered the ears. She looked at me with a pair of dull, washed-out blue eyes, as if she didn't see very well. When I nodded and smiled, she smiled back, showing a set of yellowish choppers. I saw she was wearing a long, plain dress — or long for her, at least — that was the same color of green as the inside of a water trough. She wore flat shoes and heavy socks that hung down on the ankles.

"Afternoon," I said.

She smiled again, and as she looked up

at me I could see that her teeth were short but not narrow, like the teeth of some Indian women I had seen.

When she didn't answer, I thought for a second that maybe she didn't know how to talk. So I spoke again. "Nice day, even if it's a little warm."

"Oh, it's just fine," she said, in a voice that surprised me by being so normal.

"Do they give you all the hard work?"

"I don't know," she said. "All I know is there's always work to do."

"Isn't that the truth? I think it's the same everywhere you go."

"Some people get a day off. But I never do. I have to do everything. They say they need me every day and wouldn't be able to find someone to fill in for me if I took a day off."

"I guess that's not all bad. It makes you out to be important, anyway."

"Oh, I don't know," she said, wrinkling her nose. "But I know they don't have anyone else to do what I do."

"I see. Are you the only working girl here, then?"

She smiled with her mouth closed and gave what I was beginning to see as an empty look. "That's right."

"Well, then I can believe you keep pretty

busy and don't get much of a chance to fall into idleness."

"Oh, I stay busy," she said. "Serve the meals and do the dishes, sweep and mop and clean the rooms." She looked up at me and smiled, showing her short broad teeth.

I felt she was trying to get my approval, so I said, "That's all good work." Then I had a thought. "Say, I know of a fellow who's lookin' for kitchen work. Do you think they'd want to put someone on?"

"Oh, no. I don't think so. I've mentioned it, but they say, 'We have just enough work for you, Iris.' Then they turn around and tell me I can't have a day off because they can't find anyone to fill in. So they want to be both ways about it, but I don't complain. I just do my work. I do everything. Serve the meals and do the dishes, sweep and mop and clean the rooms."

"Oh, do you have a lot of rooms to clean?"

"Just seven right now. But even if they had all the rooms full, they wouldn't get someone else. They'd say, 'We have just enough work for you, Iris.' "

"I see. So you don't have all that many people staying here."

"It's still work. Carryin' a mop bucket up and down the stairs."

"Oh, I have no doubt. They'd be in a pretty fix if they didn't have you. By the way, is there a whole family that lives here and runs the place?"

A man's voice came from the doorway. "Iris, you'd better finish up there and come get started in the kitchen."

She smiled at me with her mouth closed again, but she didn't look so vacant. The way she had her head up reminded me of a puppy, looking to be petted. "Well, I've got to go," she said. "That's Warlick." She turned around and carried her broom inside.

I waited for a few seconds, not sure whether to turn around or go forward. In that instant, the man appeared out of the doorway. It was the same scowling fellow I had seen the day before, the gloomy one with the stooped shoulders. He must have taken the broom from Iris, as he held it in his right hand as if he was going to do something pretty important with it.

I nodded to him, and he gave me a stonewall look, as if to say he didn't need to talk to the likes of me, who came around pestering his help. I thought he looked like the type that would kick a dog without much of a reason.

As I turned away I noticed all in a glance

94

his thick eyebrows and dark stubbled face, his heavy build, the dark jacket and vest, and the glint of a watch chain. I remembered Chanate saying that this fellow wasn't a real hunchback, and I remembered the superstitious part as well, about rubbing the hump. I didn't think there would be any good luck at all in touching Warlick.

I had the feeling, as I walked back to my horse, that I had come a little closer to seeing the girl again, even if one of her keepers had met me at the gate. When I count my weaknesses, they are always the same — pretty women, good food, and relaxing drink. If I wanted to add to my list of weaknesses, I would have to think of things that gave me less pleasure but still raised a reaction in me. Maybe I would make it into a second list, and pretty close to the top I would put people telling me I couldn't do something. That is, something I didn't see as having anything wrong with it. This fellow Warlick, then, went into the same category as Rudd and Whitlow, and since the thing he was trying to keep me from doing was alive and had some tug to it, all he made me do was think of another way to get close to it.

So I went to the Jack-Deuce to think

things over and to see if I might get some kind of help. I had the idea that the down-and-out newcomer, Goings, might be able to get in the door of that boardinghouse for a few minutes at least. And I thought that Tome might have picked up something, being, as he was, sort of a magnet for little filings of knowledge that dropped here and there.

Once inside the saloon, though, I didn't see either of them. I stood at the bar and took my time, drinking a glass of beer and then another. I didn't have a clear idea of how I was going to talk Goings into doing something on my behalf, but I thought that if I got to talking to him, something might shape up. But he didn't show, and neither did Tome. I was left to my own devices, as they say, and by the time I finished my second beer I decided I was going to have to go give it another try myself.

I had no idea of what kind of a schedule they kept in the boardinghouse, but I remembered Warlick telling Iris to get busy in the kitchen, which probably meant getting ready for a meal. With some logic and the help of the two beers, I thought it might be a good time to take a peek out back, if some of the folks were going to be busy up front.

Outside the saloon, I saw that the sky was clouding up in the west. Knowing how a summer shower could build up at this time of day, I wondered what to do with my horse. I didn't want him in my way, making noises, if I was snooping around back of the boardinghouse, and I thought he would make a good decoy if someone like Rudd came along again and wanted to make assumptions about where I was. I looked at the sky for a long moment and decided I would leave the horse where he was. Even if it rained, there was a good chance I would be back by then.

Sundown was still a long ways off, but with the sun behind the clouds, the day was darkening. I had a sense that sounds brought more attention when the light faded, so I took off my spurs and put them in my saddlebag. Then I set off on foot in the direction of the side streets.

In order to stay clear of the front door and windows of the place, I took a round-about route. I turned in one block early, walked to the first corner, caught a cross street, and came around in back of the building. There I saw the same outbuildings I had seen from the street. One looked like an outhouse, where I imagined Iris dumped the thunder mugs, and the other looked like a shed or low stable. It had a double door held together with a chain and lock. I stood in front of it for a couple of minutes, wondering what was inside, and then I went up to the crack between the two doors and squinted my right eye into the darkness.

A voice behind me made my shoulders jerk.

"Are you looking for someone?"

I figured I was caught, but I turned around as calm as I could. And I'll be damned if it wasn't Iris herself, the *enanita*. Her normal voice had thrown me again.

"I don't know," I said. "Is there anyone to be looking for?"

She gave me her blank look as she turned her face up and showed her little teeth. "Not out here."

"I was wonderin' what was in the shed."

"Just some stuff that Warlick keeps."

"Oh, I see." I smiled down at her. "The way they keep you so busy, I'm surprised you had a minute to come outside."

"I came out to toss a bucket of dirty water, and when I saw you, I thought I'd come over here first. I didn't know what you were looking for."

It occurred to me that she didn't see anything wrong or suspicious about me being there, so I decided not to let on that I'd been caught at anything. I thought it would be better to act as if everything was as familiar as could be. "Oh, it's hard to tell." I lifted my chin and looked toward the house. "Sounds like Maud and Warlick don't give you any rest."

"Not much, between the cleaning and the meals and the dishes."

"I suppose you're gettin' up close to the supper hour."

"Not for a little while. But I got the potatoes peeled."

"Well, that's good." I looked at her and wondered how old she was. She had to be somewhere between twenty and thirty, but she acted like a child. "Tell me, what does a girl like you get to do when you get some time off?"

"Not much, and it doesn't happen very often."

"But there must be something you like to do."

"Oh, I don't know." She had the puppy-dog look again, as if she was happy that someone took the trouble to pet her.

I felt guilty for just a second, as if I was taking advantage of her, and then I pushed that feeling aside as I thought of Helen. This was just a means to an end.

"Well, there must be something you like," I said.

"I like ice cream."

"Is that right? You know, there's a couple of places here in town where you can order some and eat it right there."

"I know."

I took a breath and drew my shoulders back. "I'd invite you to go have some, but I know how Maud and Warlick are."

"Oh, they wouldn't let me."

"I know. But you could probably go by yourself, couldn't you?"

She tipped her curly head to one side and then the other. "Oh, I guess so."

"I tell you, it would be nice if you could do that. Even if I wasn't there, you could remember me as the fellow that cares about a working girl." I slipped a quarter out of my pocket and offered it to her.

"Oh, no. I couldn't do that."

"Ah, come on. It's just from me to you, and that's all there is to it. You don't even have to tell anyone you know me. Just enjoy the ice cream — or really, whatever you want."

"I don't think I can."

I put on a frown. "Just because it's me? I bet the gentlemen give you a little bit of a tip now and then."

"Yeah, they do. But that's usually for something I do."

"Like a towel, or water, or something?"

She nodded. "Things like that."

I held out the coin to her again. "Here, take it, and I'll think of some little errand you can do."

Her right hand wavered at her side. "I don't know what it would be, and I need to get back inside, or one of 'em will come lookin' for me."

"They should treat you better, Iris. But here, take it. And I'll tell you what. You can take a message to someone."

"Who's that?"

I gave her a soft wink. "Helen. You can tell her I'm the boy she met yesterday, and I'd really like to see her again. I can wait out here for a while, or I can come back. Does she come down for supper?"

"No, I take it up to her room. Maud 'n' Warlick don't let the girls eat with the men that take their meals here."

"Well, that's just perfect. You can tell her those few words when you take supper to her. Or you could tell her before that. What do you think would be best?"

"I don't know."

I held out the quarter with the tips of my thumb and finger at the very edge of it. "If it's all the same to you, then, maybe you could tell her before supper. That way I wouldn't have to wait so long."

She reached up her hand, and I saw that her fingertips were nubby, as if the nails had been chewed way back. She took the coin.

"All right," she said. "But I can't let Maud 'n' Warlick know."

"Absolutely not." I smiled to myself as much as to her. The way she pronounced the names of the two jailers together, it sounded like a word out of *Frankenstein*. "This is just between us," I said. "Mum's the word. And as far as that goes, Maudenwarlick don't even talk to me."

I stood there for quite a little while, it seemed, as the shadows got longer and the air got cooler. It felt as if we were going to get some rain, and I was hoping I wouldn't have to stand in a downpour wondering if the girl was going to show.

When I was at the point of deciding how much longer to wait, I saw the back door of the boardinghouse open inward, and a normal-sized blond girl stepped out. It was Helen.

My heart gave a couple of quick thumps as I waved. She made a low wave in return and came my way at a fast walk. I noticed she was wearing the same dress as the day before, and I thought her shape looked just as good. She didn't say anything until she was close enough to speak in a low voice.

"Let's get in back of this thing," she said, nodding toward the shed.

When we were in back, I said, "I'm glad you could make it. I wasn't sure if you would want to come or even if you would remember me."

"I thought it was you. Iris said it was some boy I met yesterday, and you were the only one I could think of."

"That's what I told her to say. I thought it would sound more innocent."

"Oh, I don't think she has much of a sense of what goes on anyway."

"She seems nice enough."

"Yes, but she gets tiresome. She says the same things over and over again."

I smiled. "How many times did she have to tell you about me?"

"Oh, just once. But I had to wait a little while to make sure things were clear."

"Good idea. I don't think Maud or Warlick, either one, cares for me very much."

"Warlick hasn't said anything."

"Well, he's seen me a couple of times,

and he gives me dirty looks. Has Maud said something?"

"Oh, she just said I shouldn't be talking to saddle tramps."

I flinched. "She called me that?"

"She talks about everyone that way."

"I can imagine. She seemed pretty brassy to me." I took a deep breath and let it out, trying to settle myself into the conversation I wanted to have. "Anyway, I'm glad you could come out for a few minutes."

She seemed to be searching for something in my face as she said, "I am, too."

"They seem to keep a pretty close eye on you."

"Yes, they do."

I looked toward the house and back at her. "I don't know how much time we have, so I guess I'd better not beat around the bush. Ever since I saw you yesterday, I haven't wanted to do anything but see you again, and I was hoping you would want to see me."

"Well, I guess I did." She looked down.

I touched her left hand with my right, and as she looked up I said, "Helen, I have this feeling that — By the way, Helen *is* your real name, isn't it?"

"Yes, it is."

"And is that woman really your aunt?"

She looked down again. "Well, no, not really."

I let out a breath. "That was what I was about to say. I have this feeling that these people are holding you, that you aren't really free."

She looked at me and shrugged. "Something like that."

"But you couldn't tell me that yesterday when she was there."

"I guess not."

I looked at the house again and back at her. "I don't know how much to ask, but I know I want to see you again."

She nodded.

"So I need to ask something, so I'll know what I'm up against."

"Go ahead and ask, then, and if I can answer I will."

"Well, to begin with, you aren't really free to come and go if you please, and if these people are holding you, I suppose I need to ask who they are or what business they have."

"They have a boardinghouse."

"I know that, but I mean what business they have keeping you like they do."

She shrugged again.

I hesitated and then took the plunge.

"Do you work for them?"

"No, not at all."

I paused. "Then it's got me beat. How can they just hold you there?"

"I don't know how much I can tell you, or how much I should."

"Well, these are the people who are keeping me from seeing you or talking to you, so anything you can tell me will help. And that's assuming that you want to see me, which I suppose you do, or you wouldn't have come out here."

"I do, and I don't. Or — I don't want to get you in trouble."

I shrugged it off. "You're not going to get me into any trouble. I can take care of myself. So go ahead and tell me what you can about these two characters and what they're up to. If they're not related to you, what are they doin' keepin' you all tied up?"

"They work for someone else."

"Oh." I waited for a few seconds and then said, "Someone with a name, I'd imagine."

"Um, yes."

"Well, if it's a name you can say, it gives me a lookout. Whether I know the name or not."

She held her teeth against her lower lip for a moment and then said, "They work for a man named Darcy Melva."

I shook my head. "Don't know him. Never heard of him."

"He doesn't come around very much."

"Hmmm. A stranger to me. But like I said, it gives me something to be on the lookout for."

She nodded. "I don't want you to get into trouble because of me."

"Oh, I won't."

She had a serious look on her face as she said, "You could if you're not careful."

"Oh? Is this Darcy fella dangerous?"

"I don't know, but I think he could be. Not to me, but to someone else."

"Like little old Jimmy Clevis."

She flinched.

"What's the matter?"

"Oh, nothing. It's just something you said."

"My name?"

"Yes."

"Oh. Have you heard something about me?"

"No, not really. It just reminds me of someone else."

I felt a chill creep across my shoulders. "Another Jimmy?"

She moved her head up and down without speaking.

"Jimmy Rooks?"

"Yes."

"You knew him?"

Her eyes were watery as she looked at me. "Yes, I did."

"I see. And you think he got into trouble because he knew you?"

"I don't know. But I was very upset to hear that . . . something had happened to him. Did you know him?"

"I sure did. He was my friend."

Her tears splashed on the front of her dress, on the crest of her bosom. "Do you know why it happened? If you do, will you tell me?"

"I wish I knew, but I don't."

She held her hands up in front of her face for a minute and then took them away. "I think it's terrible the way people say unkind things about a person, especially when he's gone."

"Oh, did someone say something about Jimmy?"

"Maud did."

I felt a little sting. "Did she call him a saddle tramp, too?"

"No, but she said he might have done some crooked things and gotten caught at some of them."

I thought she was trying to sound me

out as to whether I knew of anything Jimmy had done. Saying I did would be as much as pointing a finger at myself, so I played it close and said, "A man can get in trouble for things he did or didn't do."

"Well, I don't want to think bad about Jimmy. He was good to me."

"There was nothing wrong with him," I said, feeling a twinge of guilt for not being able to say anything better. Then a thought clicked. "Say, were you looking for him when I saw you on the street?"

"Yes. That was before I heard what happened to him."

"Hmm. I sort of had a hunch you were lookin' for someone, but I wouldn't have guessed it was him."

"He was supposed to meet me the day before, and he didn't come. I was starting to panic."

"With good cause, as it turns out. I'm sorry you've had to go through all the worry. But I'm glad to know there was at least one other person who cared about him."

Her eyes were brimming again. "Jimmy was the only person who was ever nice to me."

I took both her hands in mine. "I'm sorry for you, Helen. I'm sorry for you, and I'm sorry for Jimmy. He was my friend. And he doesn't have to be the last person to ever be nice to you."

She blinked her eyes a few times and cleared them. "You're not afraid?"

"Maybe I should be, but I'm not. I want to find out what happened to Jimmy, and if I can help you at the same time, why, so much the better." I felt brave at the moment but also a little false, because I knew what most of my motive was in wanting to comfort this girl.

"Be careful," she said.

"Do you want me to help you?"

"If you want to."

I still had both her hands in mine, and as I looked into her eyes I felt that she was asking me not to leave her to the mercy of these people who held her. I took her to me, and she met me in a kiss. We released, then moved closer for a second, longer kiss. I put my arms around her and felt her move into me with the shape of her body fitting mine.

Raindrops were starting to fall, first a few and then more — heavy raindrops, the kind that come with a good shower.

As we drew apart she smoothed her hair and said, "I have to go."

"All right," I said. My voice sounded

husky to me, and I felt keyed up. "I'll be back."

"Thank you," she said. "Thank you." Then she turned and ran through the falling rain, back to the boardinghouse and the watchful eyes of Maud and Warlick.

I admired her figure as she ran and then went up the steps into the building. There was a lot to her, I thought, but she wasn't free to share it with someone like me. Not yet, anyway. From the sounds of it, she had fallen into the hands of someone called Darcy Melva, whoever he was. I realized she was like the ripe peach that rolled down the board. I could see the peach, clear as day, nudged off its stem and then rolling. This Darcy fellow was the one who held the board, but all I could see of him was his hands.

Chapter Six

The rain started coming down heavier, so I ran through the back of the lot to a stable behind one of the buildings that faced Main Street. I stood beneath an overhang and waited out the downpour, which lasted for about ten minutes. The back of my shirt was wet, but my trousers weren't too bad, and my pistol had just a few drops on it. I'm always conscious of things that shouldn't get wet, and I had held my hand over the butt end of the gun as I ran for shelter. Then, as I waited for the shower to pass, I thought about my horse standing in front of the Jack-Deuce. It wouldn't be the first time that my saddle and bridle had gotten wet, but I had the sense of being a touch irresponsible, off trying to play kootchie-koo with a girl when my horse was tied up in the rain. At the same time, I knew there wasn't much I could do to change things. By the time I could get back there, the horse would be wet anyway, and all I would have done would be get myself soaked as well. So I stood in a sheltered place and watched the rain fall.

It wasn't a bad way to spend ten minutes. The curtain of water shut me out from the rest of the world, and I was free to appreciate something as simple as rain. They say it falls on the just and the unjust alike, which I sometimes wonder about, but from where I stood I could at least get the impression that it was giving Monetta a pretty even drenching. Then it let up, and the air was fresh and clean, with that extra charge of energy that comes with a passing storm. I realized I had a surge from meeting up with Helen, too, and I had a spring in my step as I walked back to the Jack-Deuce.

My horse didn't seem any worse for the shower. He smelled about normal for the circumstances — like a wet horse with a wet wool saddle blanket. I patted him and told him what a good boy he was, and then I went into the saloon.

Inside I found the air stale and the light dim. I called for a glass of beer and stood at the bar, looking around. There at the same table where I had seen them the day before sat Tome and Goings. When my beer came, I took it with me and wandered toward their table.

"How go the wars?" asked Tome.

"Normal. Mind if I sit down?"

"Please do."

I nodded to him and Goings as I set my beer on the table. They were both dry and composed, so I guessed they had made it into the saloon before the rain came. Goings looked so dry, in fact, that I didn't think he had had much water touch him at all since the last time I had seen him. Tome looked neat and groomed, as usual.

"What's new?" I asked.

Tome pushed his lips out and shook his head. Goings shrugged.

"Had a nice little rain there."

"Uh-huh." Tome moved his large head up and down, and the lamplight reflected on his eyeglasses.

"Should be good for the grass," I went on. I looked at Goings and nodded. I didn't know how much he spoke the language of the country — that is, whether he knew that all good cowpunchers were supposed to praise the rain on behalf of the cattle and that all good townspeople were supposed to agree.

Goings didn't answer. He sat there with an open look on his face, and I remembered what he had said about working around horses. He hadn't said where he had been kicked, but he had the look of a man who had gotten it pretty hard in the head at one time or another. For all that he was clear-eyed and alert, he looked as if he had a dark corner somewhere, a tiny little region where the light wasn't going to shine again.

Tome spoke up. "Hear anything else about that pal of yours that got killed?"

I had to appreciate him all over again. He didn't make fun of me for acting like a simple cowpoke, but he didn't play into it, either. "I understand they were shippin' his body back to Missoura," I said.

Tome scratched his beard. "That's what I heard, too." He looked at Goings and then at me. "Sounded like your boss just wanted to sweep it away."

"Might be," I said. Then I realized he probably meant Rudd instead of Whitlow. "I guess he came by while I was sittin' in here yesterday."

"Just doin' his job." Tome picked up his pipe, which lay on the table in front of him.

"I suppose. The big boss isn't any too happy either."

Tome paused with his lips set in a matter-of-fact way. "Oh, *him*."

I looked at Goings. "My boss is a fellow named Whitlow. He's got an outfit called the Kite, and he has a few little places scattered here and there. I work at one of 'em."

Goings took a small sip of his whiskey. "He's a cattleman, then."

"Styles himself one." Tome stuck his little finger into the bowl of his pipe.

I looked at Tome. "Do you know him?"

"Know of him. He doesn't come into town much, least not in the daylight."

"Well, you probably know more about him than I do."

"I might. Did you know he uses a dead man's brand?"

"Really?" I said. "No, I didn't know that. How does he get away with it?"

"The dead man can't complain. And no one else has taken the trouble to do anything about it."

I shook my head. "Whose brand was it?"

"Oh, someone he knew up north and a ways east. Older fellow. When he up and died, Whitlow helped the widow manage things for a while. She sold off everything but the brand, and when she died, he just took it over. He had wheedled her into making him her executor, so then he had someone else's name to trade on when it suited him. After a while he moved over here and got set up on his own."

My eyes opened. "And no one does anything about it? Didn't these old folks have any kids?"

"Oh, yeah. But they're grown up and married off, and there's no money at stake, so there's not enough to fight about. And I imagine he's got 'em buffaloed, bein' the executor."

I gave it a thought. Rustling cattle was one thing, sort of clean and simple and impersonal in its own way, but this was something else. "Sounds like a kind of trespassing, I think."

"Downright cheeky, if you ask me."

"Huh. I didn't know any of this."

"I doubt that your foreman would tell you, much less the boss himself."

"I guess not. But is it pretty common knowledge?"

"Oh, not what you'd call public. But people talk. Something like this follows a man and catches up. He can't outrun a bad smell if he's got it in his own pants."

"So he did something halfway crooked there, then came here and got set up? What does a fellow like that do if more than talk catches up with him?"

"Oh, he'll go somewhere else and do something similar."

"I guess I've seen that."

"Sure. His type moves from one dirty job to the next. Those folks out east of

Fort Collins weren't the first job he pulled, either."

"Probably not."

Tome was stuffing tobacco into his pipe. Without looking up, he tossed off a casual comment. "And you won't hear it from his foreman, either, even if he knows it."

"What's that?"

"His first job."

I knew I was going to have to ask him right out. "And what was it?"

Tome's eyebrows went up as he looked at me through his spectacles and said, "Whitlow got his start by stealing sheep in Nebraska."

"The hell."

"That's his style."

"Stealin' sheep?"

"Well, that too, but I meant pulling something crooked and jumping to the next place when things get hot."

All this time I had a sense of Goings just sitting there and taking it in. I looked at him and then at Tome.

"You don't seem to worry too much about sayin' things like this out loud," I said.

"Aw, hell. His kind doesn't deal too well with the truth. If one person knows it, another does, and if he tries to do something

118

about it, it just makes for more talk. If it gets good and public, like it did in Nebraska, that's when he has to move on."

"I see. That's why he went to another state. But from Fort Collins to here, he stayed in the same state so he could keep that brand. So he must not have been in too much hot water there."

"Not enough." Tome lit his pipe.

"It makes you wonder how long he's good for around here."

"Don't get your hopes up too soon. He might keep things under the blanket for a long while yet. For the likes of me, that's not up close to any of it, it's just wait and see."

I nodded. "I think I follow you."

"And mark this," he said between puffs. "A fellow like that can't stop talk when it gets out, but he'll do whatever he can to keep people around him from saying too much."

I had an image of Jimmy Rooks in the last posture I had seen him in. "Do you think that might have anything to do with what happened to my pal?"

"No tellin'. Depends on what he might have had to say. I'd think that most of what he could have told would have been about himself as well, but I don't know."

119

I shook my head. "Neither do I." I looked at Goings and wondered how much of any of this he was following. "What do you think of all of this?" I asked.

"Stealing sheep," he said. "That's about it. I'd rather be pickin' up bones."

I didn't have an answer for that, but the mention of work made me think of something else. "By the way," I said, "I ended up meetin' that short girl that works at the boardinghouse. She says they've got her overworked but probably wouldn't hire anyone else."

"That's what I figured. Tom said it was a pretty tight couple that runs it."

Tome took his pipe out of his mouth and held it in midair as if he had something important to say. "What you ought to do is get in there and knock up that midget, and then when she gets too big to reach the dishpan, you move right in and get the job."

Goings laughed, and a light came into his eyes. "You've got the best ideas."

"Always thinkin' of my friends. We'll get you in the front door and Jimmy in the back door, and we'll have everyone purrin' like a kitten."

"Except Maud and Warlick," I said.

"Oh, those two. We'll figure out something for them."

Goings had a bright and cheerful look on his face. "Are you sure you aren't lookin' out for the old lady yourself?"

Tome pursed up his face. "That old bawd? I should say not. This is strictly altruistic. We get you a job, and we get Jimmy somethin' nuzzly."

"All in a matter of six months or so," I said.

"Uh-huh. Provided that your little kitten doesn't get herself knocked up in the meanwhile and queer that part of the deal."

"You put it all so nicely."

"Hell's bells, Jimmy. It's not a convent, you know."

I had two drinks with Tome and Goings, and when it seemed I had improved my knowledge as much as I was going to, I left the Jack-Deuce. My horse had dried off somewhat and didn't seem to mind the idea of moving on. He picked up a brisk pace as we headed south toward the plank bridge.

Over on the other side, everything was calm. It was early evening now, time for chores for those who had to do them. I remembered Tome's joke from the day before about having to milk the cow, and I was glad not to be tied down to a life of things like that and feeding the chickens. Then I remembered Goings's remark about stealing sheep, which was a bit close for comfort, and I got to thinking again about how I needed to make my move. I saw two little boys, about six or seven years old, throwing stones into a mud puddle left by the storm. I thought, *I'll never be that carefree again, but I ought to be able to get out of this life of being a thief.* Just being in Mexican town made me feel better, but I knew it was going to take more than good feelings. And I knew no one was going to do it for me, not any more than Goings was likely to lift the skirt on that midget.

I went to the butcher shop to drop in again on my friend Chanate. I doubted he had heard much more than he had the day before, but it was worth my effort. Not only that, but I thought I should stop by if I was in the neighborhood. I still felt a little guilty about not seeing him in person when I left the news about Jimmy Rooks, and I knew that at the bottom of that there was another layer of guilt. I didn't lie to these people any more than I could lie to Tome, but I couldn't talk in plain terms about the kind of work I did, and that made for pretending, which was a kind of lie. All of this would have made me much less willing to visit at all except that people like Chanate and Magdalena, who knew what I was, treated me with *confianza*. It means confidence or trust. They forgave me for what I did, and they knew I would not ever turn on them. I felt as if they knew, better than I did, that one of these days I was going to get myself straightened out.

When I walked into the meat market, Chanate was talking to two men. They wore hats and spurred boots, and their clothes were dusty. I knew them both. One of them was Quico, Chanate's nephew, and the other was Fernando, his friend who worked at the sheep camp with him. I knew that Quico brought sheep to town every week or so and killed them for his uncle, and Fernando often came along.

I always liked this young fellow Quico. He was a few years younger than I was, short and husky and good-natured. Today he was dressed as usual, with his flat-crowned hat, a red bandanna around his neck, a leather vest, a *pistola* on one hip, and a sheath knife on the other. His full mustache went up in a smile as he saw me.

His friend Fernando was likable enough, but he usually stood back, and not being related to Chanate, he gave me the impression that I was friends with the family first. He smiled a lot, too, but his eyes went everywhere, and he didn't seem to miss much. He was taller than Quico, lighter-featured and clean-shaven. He wore a plain hat with a dented crown, and he had no knife or gun in sight. To me it seemed he didn't put as much on the outside as Quico did, except for the big jingling spurs like most of them wore. He was the type that the Mexicans call serious, which means he didn't talk and laugh as much as some of them did. I figured him for a few years older than Quico, but I don't think his age had much to do with being reserved. He was just that way.

I knew that both of these fellows were hard riders. They were the kind that would work a full day, get cleaned up, ride a long ways to go to a saloon or a dance or just to walk past a girl's window, and then ride back in time for work the next day. Say what you want about Mexicans sleeping all the time, but I've known a lot of them that are night owls and go on short sleep for days at a time. Other than the habit of losing sleep, these two lads were like me, insofar as a few drinks and one or more girls were always worth the effort of looking into.

I shook hands with Chanate and his two visitors. Quico asked me how I had been and I told him fine, but as I did so I recalled that he had been on hand when the news about Jimmy Rooks went across the river.

Without saying anything more about myself, I turned to Chanate and asked if he had killed any sheep today. He said no, so I imagined the young men had come to town on some other business. No one seemed to be in a hurry to go anywhere, although all three of them were standing. I hesitated for a minute and then told Chanate I had just dropped in to say hello. I asked him to send my greetings to Clementina, and with another round of handshakes and good wishes I took my leave. I had it in my mind to visit Magdalena, so it wasn't as if I was being thrown out into the cold.

Just as I reached the door I heard a soft feminine voice, so I turned to look. There in the doorway that led from the living quarters stood a very pretty girl. She was wearing a yellow dress that struck me as being bright and clean. She had dark hair that reached halfway to her shoulders, and she had a light tan complexion. I could see at a glance it wasn't Magdalena, and as I was already on my way out, I kept going until I heard the doorbell tinkling behind me. Whoever it was, I wouldn't have minded meeting her, but the thought gave way to another that was pleasant enough.

Down the streets I rode until I came to Magdalena's little house. She answered the door and invited me in. She was wearing the same dress as the day before, and she looked just as appealing with her long dark hair hanging loose. The light inside the house was dim, or dusky, and it took my eyes a minute or so to adjust as I took off my hat and sat down. Then I could see her red lipstick, and I was happy to be in her company.

"Well, Yimi, how do you find yourself today?"

"All right, I imagine."

"Have you been working hard?"

"No, not really. It's just the same trouble, you know."

"Oh, yes. The girl. Doesn't she care for you?"

"Oh, there's that, too. Actually, I was able to see her. That's not so bad. But it's the other thing, about my friend."

"Your partner?" She used the word *compañero*, which I had used the day before.

"Yes, him. I don't know what to do about it."

"What can you do?"

"Well, I can try to find out who did it." I took a deep breath and decided to go ahead. "And the other thing that I think I can try to do is to quit working there. But I have to be careful. Do you understand me?"

"You mean in leaving the ranch?"

"Yes, that. It's not a good place, and there might be some danger if I'm not careful about the way I leave."

"Oh, yes." Then she sat up straighter and said, "But the other thing, with the girl, it goes all right?"

"I think so. I was able to talk to her for a few minutes."

"That's good."

"Uh-huh. I met the small girl first, *la enanita*. Then she told the other girl to come see me."

"Oh, how sweet. And is she nice, the *enanita?*"

"She talks a lot, and I had to give her money to buy ice cream, but she helped me. I think she's pretty innocent."

Magdalena laughed. "Oh, how cute. She likes ice cream."

"That's what she says."

"She's like a little girl."

"I think so. I don't know how much she knows about anything, but she is nicer than the hunchback."

She laughed again, still soft. "You met him?"

"Not exactly. But he guards the door. A real grouch."

She nodded as if she understood, but she didn't say anything.

I wondered if she had happened to notice, somewhere in her travels, how jealous an old whoremaster can be. However much she knew, it was bound to be a hell of a lot more than the *enanita* would ever figure out. So I said, "Tell me, Nena, what you know."

"About what?" She made a slight frown.

"Do you think the guest house is something more? Tome made a joke again today, and he made me think the girl might be — you know, something else."

"The blond girl."

"Yes. Her."

Magdalena shook her head. "I don't know, Yimi. Tome knows more. He is older, and he lives over there."

"I know. I remember you told me that before. And it was just a joke he made today."

"Does she like you, Yimi?"

"I think so. She says she wants to see me again."

"She said that?"

"Actually, I think I said I would be back, and she said it would be all right."

"I think that's good. So you'll go back, then?"

"Oh, yes. Unless it's a bad idea."

"How?"

"Well, I don't know. Maybe I won't know until later. I am very interested now, but I don't know if things will change."

"You think she might turn out to be like a rock in your shoe?"

"Maybe something like that." I didn't know how much to tell Magdalena, such as the part about the blondie girl knowing my *compañero*, because I myself didn't know how much it meant. "But here's how you can help me, if you want. If you hear any gossip about that place, or about any of the people, I would like to know."

"All right, Yimi."

"For example, I heard the owner is a man named Darcy Melva. If you happen to find out anything about him or the witch or the hunchback or the girls, it would help me."

"That's fine. How is he called again?"

"Melva. Darcy Melva. Sounds like *malvado,* doesn't it?"

"A little."

"Anyway, if you hear something, I would appreciate it."

"All right."

"Thank you, Nena. You know, sometimes I feel stupid, as if I should know more."

"Oh, you're not stupid. And even less so when you find out more."

"Thanks." I stood up with my hat in my hand, not knowing why I was always in a hurry to leave a person I liked so much. "I should go. I need to go back to the ranch."

She stood up as well, and she had a soft look on her face. "I'm sorry. I should have offered you something. Have you eaten?"

"Well, no. But I can eat when I get to the ranch."

"So you're going there?"

"Yes. I already saw the girl, and Tome, and your uncle. By the way, there was a girl in the butcher shop. I saw her, but I didn't meet her."

"Oh, that would be my cousin, Rosa Linda. She came to visit."

"Would that be Quico's sister? I saw him and Fernando there, too."

"No, she's another cousin." As Nena

shook her head, I could see she was wearing small red hooped earrings.

"And they came to town to say hello to her?"

"I imagine so."

"I barely saw her, but she looked very nice."

"She is. Maybe you can meet her later."

"Maybe so." I held out my hand, and we gave a light touch in parting. "Thank you, Nena."

"Thank you for visiting, Yimi." I saw the red earrings again, and the red lipstick and the waving dark hair, as I heard her say, "I hope everything goes well for you." It's a set phrase they use: *"Que te vaya bien."* I was used to hearing it when the bell on the door tinkled behind me in a store, and now it echoed in my mind as I heard her door close and I stood outside in the dusk of evening. All I had left to do was go back to the boar's nest. Things would be about the same there, I imagined. I would be kept on the outside, even while I sat inside, half choked with the smell of bacon grease, kerosene fumes, and tobacco smoke. It wasn't much to look forward to, but at the moment I didn't think I had much choice.

Chapter Seven

On the way back to the boar's nest, I thought some more about this fellow Darcy Melva, whoever he was. When I said his name in the middle of a Spanish sentence, it sounded a little like *malvado* but not much. I think Magdalena was just humoring me to agree even as much as she did. Now, as I rode by myself, I said his last name out loud a few times, and damned if it didn't sound like *malva*. That took some of the charm out of it. The word *malvado* means "evil" or "wicked," like the stepmother in the fairy tale — *la malvada madrastra*. And poor *malva* is just a weed that grows around the farmyard, a low-lying weed at that. So there it was. I had to wonder what I should think of someone who had a name that means weed.

Even that amusement didn't last long. The closer I got to the boar's nest, the less the world seemed like a place where people said and did funny things. Except for their sarcasm, Rudd and Turner were a pretty humorless pair. If I was going to find anything to lighten the air, I figured I was going to have to do it on my own. I smiled at one possibility. Maybe I could get Turner to talk about the time the dark brother tried to choke him to death.

It was getting on to dark when I rode into the line camp. I expected someone to say something about my getting back so late, but neither of them mentioned it. They no doubt heard me when I rode into the yard, so when I walked into the shack after putting my horse away, no one showed any surprise. Rudd was sitting at the table smoking a cigarette, with his right stovepipe boot hiked up on his left knee. He looked over and nodded when I said hello. Turner had his back to me as he stirred a pot on the stove.

"Cookin' beans?" I called out.

He rapped the big spoon on the lip of the pot. "Uh-huh."

"What's new?" I asked, walking over toward him.

He looked around. "Nothin'. Nothin' at all."

Rudd's voice came up from in back of me. "How about yourself, Clevis? What did you see?"

"Nothing new, really." As I said it, I realized I had seen a couple of things I hadn't seen before — one being the *enanita* and the other being Rosa Linda — but I didn't see any convenient way of telling Rudd that. I sniffed the air. Even if it was just beans, it was good for a change. And I was hungry. I had missed out on getting anything to eat in Mexican town. I didn't have any right to expect a meal there, but I sure wouldn't have turned one down, especially after I'd made quick work of noon dinner just to get away from the line camp. But no one offered, so here I was, back at robbers' roost and ready to share the vittles.

Turner dipped the spoon into the pot and lifted a little mound of beans to his mouth. He blew away the steam, slurped the juice, then poked the tip of the big spoon into his mouth. I hoped, for his sake and ours, that it had been a while since he had cut himself a chew.

"What would we think of some biscuits?" I asked.

Turner stuck the spoon back in the pot. "Oh, I don't care. For all the trouble they take, this is good enough."

I looked at Rudd, who had turned his cigarette sideways and was looking at it.

"I don't care either," he said. "You're just eatin' to make a turd anyway."

I sure had a better opinion of eating than that, and I felt like saying something, but I let it go. I didn't know if Rudd was trying to get under my skin or if a decent meal just didn't rank any higher in his scale of things. I decided it didn't matter. I was going to get out of this place as soon as I could anyway, and I didn't care to find out whether I was being baited or not.

Supper came off the stove not too long after that. No one said much as we ate our grub, and I got the feeling that both of them knew something and we weren't going to talk about it. I looked at Turner, his stubbled jaws bulging as he chewed sideways and made slow work of swallowing. Then I looked at Rudd, whose thin mustache moved up and down as he worked on his food. I've never been one to begrudge someone else a meal or even to dislike someone for the way he ate his grub, but I found myself resenting these two fellows for their very presence. And since all they were doing was eating, I found myself getting irritated by the way they did it. Finally I had had enough of the silence, so I spoke.

"I wonder what kind of funeral they're plannin' for Jimmy, or if they're plannin' anything at all."

"No tellin'," Rudd said.

"Huh. Seems to me that no matter what

kind of a life a fellow has led, he deserves a decent burial. He ought to have the chance to have a preacher say a few words."

Turner spoke out. "It wouldn't make any difference to me if I was the one in the box."

"Of course it wouldn't," said Rudd. "You'd be way past thinking about it."

"Well, what I mean is, it doesn't make any difference now as far as what things would be like then. Some preacher talkin' ain't gonna change anything."

"It wouldn't do any harm," I said. "It just seems to be more fitting."

"Probably fits some people better'n others," Turner went on. "It's like when they say if the shoe fits wear it. It wouldn't matter to me, because I don't care about any of that."

"It still doesn't do any harm," I said, "havin' a preacher."

Turner sniffed. "I guess that depends. Some of the biggest hypocrites I've known are real goody-goodies that go to church."

"Aw, hell," I said, "that's like sayin' whiskey's no good because you've known hypocrites that drank it." I looked at Rudd, who seemed to be staying out of it.

Turner came right back. "As far as that goes, I *have* known some good churchgoers that keep a bottle stashed, and then they go on about how bad the rest of us are. That's your do-gooders for you. Don't do this and don't do that. We're better than you are. Someone that shaves every day and puts on a clean boiled shirt, and he thinks you're not as good because you don't do things the same way."

"Even if you've got stuck-up people there, that doesn't mean they're hypocrites or that there's anything wrong with church."

"Maybe so, maybe no. But for as much as they go on about how you shouldn't drink, I know one thing. They even drink wine in church."

Now Rudd chimed in. "I didn't know they had anything but moonshine where you come from."

Turner was from Kentucky, and he didn't mind mentioning it himself when it had something to do with being crude or backward, but if someone else brought up his home state in that way, he took it as if someone had kicked his coon dog, and his accent came on good and strong. "Ah didn't just fall off the turnip wagon yesterday," he said. "I know there's churches where people drink wine."

I knew of some, too, I thought, and I had

even been there when they said everything in Latin and rang the little bell for everyone to kneel or get up. But I wasn't going to drag those people, which included my good friends like Chanate and Magdalena, into what was shaping up as a stupid argument. "I don't think they see it as drinking wine," I said. "It's not like they fill their glass or get to have seconds."

Turner swelled up as if he had won the argument. "That's my whole point. They criticize others for drinking, then they do it themselves, in church, and then they say they don't do it."

I thought we'd gotten a long ways away from where we started, which was the question of whether a man deserved a few words before they covered him up. "Well," I said. "That's a good thing about freedom of religion. No one has to do any of it."

"That's right," Turner answered. "So when it comes time to plant me, you let the preacher save his breath."

"I'll remember that," said Rudd. "Then I won't have to worry about whether to tip him."

"Save that, too. Spend it on a good drink. The way I see it, when you're dead, you're dead. Like a fly."

Rudd didn't say anything more, and I

was surprised he didn't try to get in the last word like he often did. I wondered if he was bored with making fun of Turner or whether he thought he had done enough of it in front of me, and I realized I didn't care much about that either. Knowing I was on my way out of that place made it easier for me to deal with those fellows.

In the morning, Rudd told me I had to ride over to the Kite on an errand. He said the boss wanted me to deliver a couple of horses that Jimmy Rooks used to ride. By now I could see the pattern of how Rudd told me things and when, and I didn't like it.

So I said, "Why didn't the boss take 'em himself when he was just here?"

Rudd tensed his thin little mustache. "I didn't ask him."

It sounded like an echo. I remembered he had given me the same answer before. As I took it in, I realized I was being told it was not my place to ask questions when I was given my orders. So I kept my mouth shut, and not long after breakfast I left the two of them sitting at the table as I went about my business of getting ready to go on my errand.

I went out and caught the two horses

139

Rudd spoke of, a sorrel and a bay. I left them tied at the hitching rail and then went and got the one I planned to ride for the day. It was a light brown horse I hadn't ridden in a week or so. As I led him to the rail, it occurred to me that my horse would be fresher for the ride back if I rode one of Jimmy's on the way over. So I saddled the sorrel. As I was pulling up the front cinch, with the stirrup hooked up on the saddle horn, the idea crossed my mind that I could just as well take a saddle gun.

Mine was in a scabbard underneath my bunk, so I went in and fetched it. Rudd was still sitting by the table smoking a cigarette, with his black boot hiked up, and he gave me a looking-over as I walked to the door.

"I remembered I wanted to be on the lookout for deer," I said.

"Lot of trouble when we can have all the beef we want," he said. Then he sniffed and took a pull on his tight little cigarette.

I felt like asking him why in the hell we were eating hog meat all the time, but I figured he would have an answer that would remind me of my place again, so I said nothing. I went out and strapped the scabbard onto the left side of the saddle so it would ride beneath my stirrup fender. I expected either Rudd or Turner to come to the door and say something before I rode away, but no one showed. I rode out of the yard, mounted on the sorrel and leading the other two horses.

I rode west with the morning sun at my back. I liked the feel of the sun's warmth across my shoulders, and I also liked the feel of the saddle gun beneath the lower part of my left leg. I didn't have as much interest in a deer as I might have had a couple of days earlier, but it was a good-enough explanation to give Rudd. I couldn't see telling him I was still on the lookout for anything I could learn about Jimmy Rooks getting killed, and I sure couldn't see telling him I didn't like the way things were stacking up at the boar's nest.

As for Jimmy getting killed, I wondered if it had anything to do with his knowing that girl Helen. If it did, then I had two sides to look out for. She didn't seem to have a very strong notion as to why he got done in, but I didn't want to cross out any possibilities. It could have something to do with our side of things, the work we did for Whitlow and the Kite, but it might have had some connection with her side, and there might be more to it than she knew.

There was damn sure more to it than I knew, and I was glad to have a saddle gun under my leg and a six-gun on my hip. I told myself I needed to stay focused on my plan of getting away from the Kite in the safest way possible, and I realized that my interest in the girl might be distracting me, at least for the time I spent trying to get close to her. And I knew I wanted to get closer. That was a bold thought that gave a fellow a bold feeling under a morning sun.

I rode into the Kite at a little before noon. It was the first time I had seen the place, though I had known where it was located and had ridden in the vicinity before. Now as I approached it, it looked like any other set of run-down ranch buildings. All the lumber was weathered, with a warped board here and there trying to pull loose from its nails.

The ranch house had a roofed-over entry that was closed in on the sides and open in front. I tied up all three horses to the hitching rail and walked through the passageway to the front door. I noticed on the left wall an assortment of traps and chains and such, and a few frames for stretching pelts. On the right side hung various pieces of harness, such as leather straps, trace chains, and singletrees. I guessed all that stuff came with the place, as it was pretty dusty, and I had the feeling that at one time there were men here who did honest work.

I knocked on the door with three raps, and after a minute or so I gave it four more. Then I heard footsteps, and the door opened. Whitlow was standing inside, in the gloom.

"Come on in," he said.

He led the way through a sort of cloak-room, where I imagined the men who worked with the traps and harnesses would have left their winter coats and boots. I followed the boss into a sitting room, where the light was better. I noticed he was wearing his frock coat, as usual.

"Sit down," he said, pointing at a wooden chair with armrests and a spindle back.

I took off my hat and sat down. He sat in a chair that was a sturdier version of mine, with a padded seat. He sat about five feet from me, not quite straight on. The light was good enough that I could see his deep blue eyes. I could also see his watch chain, which I had caught a glimpse of the day he came to the line camp. It was a tawny-colored, braided chain, such as some people make of horsehair. It had a gold link on each end — one end that hung on the button of his vest and the other that connected to a leather fob that I imagined he used to pull the watch out of his vest pocket. It was a detailed little outfit he had, and it seemed protected by his neat, clean hands, which he kept folded together and resting on his belt buckle.

I looked up at his face and could see him practicing his glare on me.

"So tell me what you know about Jimmy Rooks."

I held my hat with one finger inside the sweatband, and I could see I wasn't shaking at all. "I don't really know that much," I said. "Nothing more than I said the other day."

"That's not true," he said, with a hard set to his mouth.

"I don't know what else I can tell you."

"You're the one that found him, aren't you?"

"Well, yes."

"Then tell me about that."

"I found him lying in the rocks, dead."

"Shot? Clubbed? Stabbed?"

"He had a bullet hole in him."

"Was he armed?"

I nodded. "He was still wearing his gun."

"And did it look like someone shot him

there, or shot him somewhere else and took him there?"

"It looked as if someone had dumped him there." I had the sense that I had told the boss some of this before, but I just went ahead and answered his questions. I had nothing to lie about anyway, and I didn't care if I repeated myself.

"And why there?"

"I don't know. Maybe so I could find him. I was supposed to meet him there."

"Oh, uh-huh. You think someone could have gotten that out of him before they plugged him?"

"I don't know. Depends on who it was, I guess, and how long they talked. Or they could have been watchin', and seen him comin' from one direction and me from the other."

"Wouldn't you have heard the shot, then?"

"Oh, I don't know. It's just an idea. They could have seen each of us from a long ways off and gotten to him without my hearing it. I guess there's a lot of ways they could have done it." All of a sudden I had the feeling that Whitlow was making me feel that I was under suspicion, and I realized I was speculating just to get myself off the hook when I wasn't even on it. And it occurred to me that he was doing it just to see what he could get me to say. That helped me draw in a little. "I don't know who did it," I said, "or how. All I know is I found him."

Whitlow bored his eyes at me. "Everyone knows more than they think they do. You know that?"

"I don't know what I know, really."

"Well, let me ask you this. Do you think one man did it, or more than one?"

I took a breath and exhaled. "I would say one man, at least the part where they dumped him in the rocks. I saw two sets of horse tracks coming in and going away." I shrugged. "But if they shot him somewhere else, which I think they did, it could have been more than one. And even at that, I don't know what difference it would make."

"I just like to know as much as I can."

"So do I, but it seems to me it would be awfully hard to figure out who did this until we know why."

"That's what we're coming to."

"Oh?"

"Uh-huh. I think you might know why someone would want to kill him."

I felt a chill creep across my shoulders and the back of my neck. "I already told you I didn't know anything like that."

"I know. But it's like I said. A man knows more than he thinks he does."

I shook my head. "I don't know what else there would be."

"Well, think about it. Was there anything he said, anything you noticed that was different, or anything you heard anyone else say?"

I thought of Helen and slammed that door fast. "No, not that I can recall."

He gave his head a slight shake. "There's got to be something."

I felt the conversation relax a little, and I let my eyesight drift. I saw his braided watch chain again, and his vest, and his frock coat. Beyond him I saw the clutter of his living quarters, with newspapers and dirty dishes stacked on the table and clothes piled on the floor. In just that second or two I recognized something I had noticed before, and that was that Whitlow, in spite of being clean almost to the point of being prissy, seemed comfortable in the midst of a slovenly place.

His voice brought me back. "You and him were pretty good friends, weren't you?"

"Yes, we were."

"Then I would think he would have said

something, at one time or another. Maybe just a word he dropped."

I twisted my mouth and shook my head again. "I can't bring a thing to mind."

Now he glared at me again. "You know, Clevis, I haven't liked any bit of this."

"I understand that."

"And I wish you'd ransack that little mind of yours, and if you think of anything at all that you saw or heard, you either tell me or you tell someone who can get it back to me. Do you understand that?"

"Yes, I do."

"And get this." He pointed at me with his index finger. "I don't want to find out that anyone held out anything. I think we talked about this before. You don't cross this outfit."

I nodded.

"You've got that?"

"Yes, I do."

"Well, I don't have a hell of a lot more to talk about, and you've got a ride back." He made a motion with his head in the general direction I had come from.

I stood up with my hat in both hands. I felt he was going to say something else to release me, but he just stood up and tipped his head toward the door. Then, as I went to take a step, his voice stopped me.

"Before you go, tell me something."

I turned. "What's that?"

His voice wasn't as harsh now. "Did you have anything you wanted to ask me?"

I was tempted to catch him way off guard and ask him, from out of nowhere, if he knew anything about a fellow named Darcy Melva. But something inside warned me. I had the feeling again that Whitlow was just trying to draw me out, trying to get me to say something that would tell him more. So I let my question settle back in the shadows as I thought of a simpler one.

"Actually, I do."

"And what's that?"

"I was wondering why we don't eat any more beef than we do. Rudd says we can eat it anytime we want, but it seems to me all we've had to eat is salt pork and bacon and spuds and beans. Not that I'm complainin', but I do like beef, and it doesn't cost anything."

Whitlow patted me on the shoulder. "Axel's just bein' careful. He has a good sense of when to kill a beef and when not to."

"Uh-huh."

"You just leave it up to him. And you

know one thing for sure. My men never go hungry."

I smiled and walked away. I knew he was speaking the truth at the moment, even if it wasn't a big habit with him. His men would never go hungry as long as there was a thief among them. And that just about went without saying. As I heard the door close behind me, I recalled what Tome had told me about Whitlow getting his start by stealing sheep. On one hand, it probably doesn't matter very much what a man steals if he does very much of it at all; but on the other hand, I was glad I could say I never stole any sheep. That was a good thought. It made it easier for me to deal with this fellow that I felt at my back.

I went out to the hitching rail and changed the saddle from Jimmy's sorrel to the light brown horse I had picked out for myself earlier in the day. Leaving the other two horses at the hitching rail, I rode east out of the Kite, and before long I was into the rolling country. I didn't have the feeling that anyone was watching me, but I still had a sense that I ought to get back to the boar's nest at the expected time today. So I rode straight home. When I got to the line camp, Rudd and Turner were loafing around in the shade of the shack. They both seemed to notice as I carried my rifle and scabbard inside, and it made me think of something else I might do for my own amusement.

I rummaged through my war bag until I found my sheath knife. If I had really intended to hunt deer I would have taken it with me on my ride, but now that I had an idea for it I took it out. It was about eight and a half inches long, with the blade taking up a little over half of that length. The handle was of a type I like on knives, hatchets, and hammers — a row of leather rings packed tight together, buffed smooth all the way around, and sealed with a shellac. I put the sheath on my belt on my left side and went outside.

There I set up a plank about a foot wide and about five feet tall, and I took to throwing my knife at it. I started out a couple of yards away and flung the knife straight a few times to get the feel of throwing it. I enjoyed the way it stuck in the plank with the end of the handle quivering. I kept practicing, moving back a couple of steps for a few throws and then a couple more, and so on, until I was about ten yards away and could stick the knife almost every time with a good hard throw. Rudd and Turner saw what I was doing, but they didn't say anything. I had the feeling that they didn't want to give me that much notice. That was all right with me. I wasn't trying to show off anyway. I just liked the feel of the knife leaving my hand and then the solid thunk when it stuck in the plank. And when I was done with my practice for that day, I liked the feel of the knife on my belt. It was like the rifle and six-gun earlier in the day. I wasn't sure what I was on the lookout for, but I wasn't going to be caught wandering around like a goose in the moonlight.

Chapter Eight

The next day I was back out on the range, doing what I usually did for the Kite, which was to keep track of the whereabouts and general condition of any livestock that did and did not carry the Kite brand. In the middle of the season like this, between the spring and fall roundups, cattle wandered on the open range. If we knew where the various cattle were, we could make a move when the boss thought the time was right.

As I went on my ride, checking into this draw and that, I got to mull over the way Whitlow and Rudd regarded me. On one hand, I resented the way they called me stupid and little and little-minded. But on the other hand, I thought it was just as well that they considered me that way. If they took me for such a fool and were so plain about it, I might be able to see something headed my way if it came from their direction. And despite the way they looked down on me, I wasn't as stupid as they might like me to be.

I also had the capacity to remember a thing or two, especially when it had to do with something that was uppermost with me. A good prospector will remember all the places where he saw a flash of color, and a good hunter will recall the spots where he saw buck deer and bull elk. For my part, I remembered the places where I had been served good meals, had downed good drinks, or had seen girls who made me stir. All day long as I rode here and there, on the lookout as I was supposed to be, I remembered what time of day Iris the *enanita* had come to the back door to pitch the dirty water.

It wasn't Iris who made me stir, of course, or that gave me the bold feelings that came and went during the drowsy part of the day. It was the girl she took the message to, the one with the shapely figure and shining eyes, the one who had given me back a full kiss when the rain was starting to fall. I wanted more. I wanted to know more about her. I wanted more kisses, and I wanted more than kisses. And so it worked out, as I went on my day's wandering, that I rode way out and circled around and ended up near Red Wind Crossing by late afternoon. With the sap still rising in me, I crossed the river and rode to town.

I tied my horse to a hitching rail in front

of a café on Main Street, about two blocks from the boardinghouse, and I slipped my spurs into the saddlebag again. Then I took a roundabout way to end up by the outbuilding where I had stood before. I didn't like the feeling of skulking around in back alleys, but I was willing to do it for the time being if it was going to help me see the girl. I listened at the outhouse to be sure no one was there, and I checked the shed to see that the lock and chain were in place. It didn't look as if anything had changed, and unless Warlick came out on an errand to fetch a lampshade or a fireplace poker, I had a good chance of not being disturbed if I just sat still.

Quite a little while passed, and nothing happened. My head started nodding, and I dozed off a couple of times. Then I came awake — I think the sound of the opening door woke me. There stood the *enanita* on the back step, getting herself set and then swinging the bucket to toss the gray water. It looked as if she was going to tumble off the step with her forward motion and shifting weight, but she didn't. She just teetered. When the bucket came back to rest and she settled into a standing posture, I whistled.

As she looked around, I could see her

squinting. Then she eased her way down the wooden steps, set the bucket on the ground, and came walking my way with a bit of a hobbling gait.

When she was within a few yards I said, "Hello, Iris."

"What do you want?" she asked, with that normal voice that always surprised me.

"I guess the same as before."

She showed her teeth as she said, "I don't think they want to hire anyone."

"Oh, I didn't mean that. It was just a small thing."

"They should, but I don't think they will. They want me to do everything."

"Well," I said, seeing that she wasn't going to get off that track right away, "my friend could use the work, even if it was just to give you relief once a week."

"He can ask, but I think they'll just turn him away."

"Maybe we'll just let it go, then." I smiled and nodded, as if we had quite a bit of confidence between us. "How about that other thing we talked about last time?"

She scraped her upper lip with her lower teeth, and her eyes had sort of a glinting look. "What was that?"

"I think you took a message for me."

She pursed her lips together, and with her head lowered so that I could see the pale furrow down the middle of her scalp where the tight curls separated and fell to each side, she raised her eyebrows and looked at me.

"I think we talked about ice cream, didn't we, Iris?"

"Yes, but I haven't gotten a chance to go have any."

"Well, I'm sorry you haven't, but that doesn't mean you couldn't go more than once when you had the chance."

She raised her head to give me a more direct look. "What do you mean?"

"Like we said before, Maudenwarlick probably wouldn't let you go with someone else, but you could go on your own, and if you had, say, more than one quarter, you could go more than one time."

She got something of a sullen look on her face. "Well, you just want me to take another message, then, don't you?"

"Not if you don't want to." I held out a quarter. "I'll give this to you anyway, Iris. I know you're a hardworking girl, and you deserve it. You've been good to me, and I appreciate it. I'm not going to treat you

157

like some of these other people do."

She just looked at me.

"Here, take it."

"I don't need it. And I don't want to get in trouble."

"Just take it. Maudenwarlick don't have to know a thing about where it came from. And they're sure not going to hear it from me. Here."

She looked at the quarter and tilted her head of curls to one side.

"Go ahead. I want you to have it."

"All right," she said, holding out her hand. When the nubby fingers closed around the quarter, she showed her teeth again in a half-smile. "Now, which girl did you want to send a message to? They're not all here today."

My heart sank. "Helen," I said, soft and low. "Just like before. Tell her the same boy wants to see her."

"All right." She blinked her eyes and bobbed her head, and then with her fist wrapped tight around the quarter, she made her scurry back to the house.

I had to wait for a long time, feeling like an escaped convict hiding by the outhouse. Maybe part of my guilty feeling came from knowing that I had wheedled the *enanita*. Here I was, Jimmy Clevis, resenting the way Whitlow and Rudd treated me like a dummy, then turning around and taking advantage of the *enanita* with her childish mind. I remembered what Magdalena said, that she was like a *niña*, a little girl. Then I had to remind myself that I hadn't done anything rude, like make fun of her to her face, and I hadn't done anything disgraceful, like take her out behind the barn. That was just in Tome's jokes. All I had done was use her a little bit to suit my purposes, and if that gave me cause for a tinge of shame, I also knew that deep down, I had some sympathy for her. Maudenwarlick weren't all that different from Whitlow and Rudd.

That thought in itself kept me awake for a couple of minutes. This girl Helen and I were in more similar situations than I might have realized. The difference was that I had more freedom to move around and do something, like sit out here by the outbuildings and wait for her, while she had to look for a moment to sneak away. That was the way things were until I could do something to change them, I thought. I wanted to see her, and I wasn't going to rest until I did. If she wanted to see me, then we could decide what we were going to do next.

That was a good way to boil things down, it seemed. You either did or you didn't. I was going to find out about this girl, and I either was or wasn't going to have more to do with her. Then, when I got that settled, I would decide how to cut my strings and get free of Whitlow and Rudd. Hers and mine were two separate worlds, I reasoned, and I was going to take care of them one after another.

Of course, for anything to happen, this girl was going to have to show up. Time was passing. The shadows were reaching out, and the air was calm like it gets at the end of the day. I started to worry that she might not come out once it got dark. For all I knew, that was when Maudenwarlick kept the closest watch on the girls. I remembered Tome saying it was something of a high-class place, for as much as Monetta would have one, and they let only certain people in the door. That might have something to do with what the *enanita* said about not all the girls being there today. If this place considered itself more elite than the regular sort of brothel where any old punkin roller could stumble in, then it might not have the standard thirty-minute limit. Maybe from time to time one of the gentleman types would escort a girl for an overnight or more. I still didn't know if Helen did any of that kind of work. She said she didn't, but I couldn't discount it, given the way she was kept under lock and key by the likes of Maudenwarlick. I had the idea that they kept her as part of their duty to the owner, but I didn't know how exclusive the arrangement was.

My thoughts rambled on in this fashion for quite a while, and I was starting to fidget over whether she was going to show at all, until I saw movement at the back door. My pulse picked up right away. It was getting on to the shank of the evening, and dusk was falling, but I could tell at first glance that the person was taller than the *enanita*. As she stepped out into the open and came down the steps, I could see her blond hair. It was Helen.

I stood up, and she came toward me at a fast walk. She was wearing a light-colored dress like the one I had seen her in before, but it was not the same dress. This one was more of a creamy color, and I wanted to touch it. Just watching her movement as she came my way made me anxious.

When she stood in front of me I took her hands in mine and looked into her blue eyes. She was looking back at me, as if she was searching for something.

"You came," she said.

"I had to."

Then we were in each other's arms, with no separation between us as we met in a long, shifting kiss.

When we relaxed and drew apart, she said, "Let's stand over there where we did before, so no one will see us."

I took her hand and walked with her to the shed and then behind it, where the house was closed off from view. I turned and took her hands in mine again.

"I was starting to worry about whether you were going to get away."

"Oh," she said with a puff of breath, "it seemed like I had to wait forever. Sometimes Maud drives me crazy, the way she hangs over me."

I kissed her again and said, "Helen, I wish I could get you away from here."

She moved her head back and forth in a slight motion. "I wish you could."

"Do you want me to?"

"I don't know. I don't know how much trouble it would be."

"You mean to do it, or afterwards?"

"Well, afterwards, I guess."

"What can they do? They don't own you."

"I know. You're right. But —"

"If they want to run someone's life, let 'em practice on Iris."

She smiled. "They do that pretty well. Poor thing."

"Well, come on, then. They can't have that much of a hold on you."

"Kiss me," she said. "Just hold me and kiss me."

I did all of that. Our bodies molded together as we clung and kissed for long moments, with short spaces in between when I would catch my breath and open my eyes to the dusk around us. I ran the fingers of both my hands through her hair, lifting it from her ears, and I kissed her on the side of her neck. It was warm. I kissed her there for another long moment and moved my right hand below her waist to the curve of her bottom. She pressed toward me. Then my hat fell to the ground and I was kissing her bosom, through the dress, and she was holding the back of my head with her right hand.

"I want you," she whispered.

We kissed again, and I laid my cheek to hers as I said, "Tonight? Now?"

"Yes."

"Do you want me to take you someplace?"

She shook her head.

I kissed her on the neck again and whispered, "I can do it here if you can."

Her lips met mine, and that was her answer.

By the time I was aware of my surroundings again, the moon had risen — a large, bright moon in the east, a couple of days short of a full moon. I lay on my back with my clothes in place, and she snuggled beside me with her head on my chest. Her dress was all smoothed out again, and I could feel that both of us were relaxed.

"You should let me take you away from here," I said.

"I don't know."

"This is no way to be. These people don't have any right to hold you prisoner."

"I know."

"So just leave."

"I don't know if I can."

"Well, hell. You're out here with me. Just don't go back."

"I have to."

"What for?" I raised my head and looked at her, but all I saw was her beautiful blond hair in the moonlight. She was keeping her face close to my chest. "What do these people have on you, anyway? What are they to you?"

She moved her head until her chin was on my chest, but she didn't look straight at me. "Nothing, really."

"Then what hold do they have on you?"

She waited a few seconds before she answered. "It's not so much that, but more like the hold that someone else has on them."

"You mean this Darcy Melva fellow."

"Yes."

"Well, what's he got on them, other than bein' the owner of the place?"

She let out a long breath. "Enough to keep them afraid and doing what he says."

"Sounds like blackmail to me."

"I suppose it is."

"You know," I said, "sometimes that can work both ways. What is it he's got on 'em?"

She shook her head. "I don't know if I should go into it."

"Aw, hell. The more I know, the more I can help you. Unless you don't want to tell me because it's about you as well."

"No, it's not that."

"Well, don't be afraid to tell on 'em. I'm sure not goin' to tell 'em you told me."

She hesitated and then said, "I don't know how much I should tell."

"Tell me as little or as much as you want."

"All right, then. What I'll tell you is just about them."

"That's fine."

"It's kind of ugly, but I didn't have anything to do with it. This is just to let you know what he has on them."

"Good enough. Go ahead."

"Well, there was a girl that worked for Maud and Warlick."

"Here?"

She shook her head. "No, in the last place. But that's why they moved here, to get away from there." She paused.

"Go ahead," I said.

She hesitated for a second and then went on. "This girl was going to have a baby, and they tried to help her get rid of it. And the girl . . . the girl died."

"Oh."

"But he had some property somewhere, and he told them where they could get rid of everything."

"You mean the girl, and whatever else."

"Yes."

"So did he help them?"

"No. As far as I know, he didn't touch it."

"I see." I nodded my head to one side and then the other. "You know, it seems to me you've fallen in with a bad bunch." I wanted to ask her what all this had to do with her being kept in jail, but I had already said I wasn't going to push it. So I said, "Is there anything else about this mess that you think you want to tell me?"

"No, not right now."

I frowned to myself. "Then I wonder what we ought to do next."

"I don't know."

I put my right hand on her hip. "I don't think I can just walk away from this, not at this point."

She snuggled closer. "I don't want you to."

"Well, then, we've got to do something. And you don't think you can just get up and walk away."

She shook her head.

An idea was forming in my mind. I thought I could just carry her away. "Do you think you could wait here by yourself for a few minutes?"

"I think so. Why?"

"I need to go check on my horse. When I get back, we'll decide what to do. You can be thinkin' on it in the meanwhile."

"All right. I can do that."

I kissed her again, and then I got up and set out for my horse. I walked fast until I hit Main Street, and then I slowed to a normal pace until I reached the hitching rail. I untied the reins and swung aboard, then put the horse into a fast walk. In less than ten minutes altogether, I had Helen in my arms again as my horse stood tied to a corn crib.

We were pressing against each other like before, and all of the energy seemed to have come back in full force. I was planting moist kisses on her neck as I rubbed her buttocks, and she was whispering, "Yes, yes."

I dropped to my knees and lifted her dress up, up in the moonlight, until I found her bloomers. I slipped them off and pressed my lips against her stomach, just above her golden zone. Then I rose to hold her in my arms again.

"Take me," she whispered. "Take me."

I wasn't sure which way she meant it. "Here?" I asked.

"Yes."

I lowered her to the ground again, and if there was anything she didn't get to do the first time, she followed through on this one. When we had finished and were lying side by side again, she clung to me and kissed me, and I could feel her tears against my cheek. I knew I wasn't going to let go of this.

"I've got to get you away from here," I said.

"I don't know." She pressed her fingernails against the upper part of my left arm. "I don't want you to leave me."

"Then come with me."

"What if I can't?"

"You can."

"I'm afraid."

I hooked my leg over hers and slipped my hand down to her hip. "Helen, I could feel you give yourself to me. You did, didn't you?"

"Yes."

"Then just follow through with it. Come with me."

"Where?"

"I've got a place."

I knew she was afraid, but I also knew I had her in my hands like a warm mass of dough. In that moment when she gave herself to me, I felt myself take possession of her, and that spell hadn't gone away. I could do what I wanted with her, so I lifted her to her feet by one hand and led her to the horse. She was trembling when she first got up from the ground, but when I pulled her up onto the horse's back behind me, she held on tight.

"Where are we going?" she asked as we

moved down the alley.

"I know some good people where you can hide out for a day or so until I get my things together and make a plan."

We rode slow and quiet, keeping in the shadows cast by the moonlight, until we came to the edge of town. Then we *thump-thump*ed across the bridge and dropped into Mexican town.

"Don't worry," I said. "These are my friends."

I kept to the back streets again until I came to Nena's house. I was disappointed to see it so dark, without the glow of a single candle light. From there I took us back to the main street and over, to Chanate's butcher shop. The store lay in darkness, but I could see lights in the back part, so I rode around to the side door. After Helen slid down, I dismounted and knocked on the door. I could hear voices inside, and it sounded as if a few people were chatting together.

Chanate opened the door and invited me in. I told him I had someone with me, and he said for both of us to come in. Helen and I stepped into the lamplight of the living room, and I took off my hat.

As I looked around and smiled, I saw Magdalena sitting at one end of the couch,

Clementina sitting at the other end, and the girl I took to be Rosa Linda sitting in the middle. Off to one side, seated on wooden chairs, were Quico and Fernando. They had their hats off but otherwise looked as if they had just ridden in from the sheep camp.

Clementina stood up and offered us something to eat. She said they had all just eaten supper but she could warm up something.

It sounded good to me, but when I looked at Helen and asked her if she cared to eat, she said no, she had already eaten. So I thanked Clementina and told her we were both fine, and she sat down.

Then, looking around the room at everyone, I introduced my friend Helen. In Spanish her name would be Elena, I explained. There was a round of smiles then, with a murmur of *"Mucho gusto,"* or "Pleased to meet you," from each of them.

I turned to Magdalena and spoke to her in Spanish — partly for the benefit of the others and partly because that was the way she and I always spoke. I knew she spoke English, and I could have addressed her that way for Helen's benefit, but I went for the broader purpose. "Nena," I said, "this is the friend I told you about, the one I wanted to help. I would like to ask if she could stay with you for a little while. A day or two."

"Of course, Yimi." She smiled at Helen and said, in English, "You come to my house. Everything is very fine there."

Helen smiled and said, "Thank you." Then she turned to me and said, "How about you?"

I raised my eyebrows, then decided it didn't matter how much these other people understood the rest of it. "I have to go back to the ranch," I said. "I need to put in a day or two there and see the best way to get loose. Then I'll come back, and we'll see where we go from there."

"Do you have to go now?"

"I ought to. They usually expect me by nightfall, and I'd just as soon not cause any commotion until I'm ready to get away."

Helen had an uncertain look on her face until Magdalena stood up, walked over to her, and spoke in English again.

"Everything is fine," Nena said, taking Helen's hand. "Yimi has to go to the ranch, but we take care of everything, and then he will come back." She turned to the others in the room and told them that she was going to take the young lady to her house.

Quico and Fernando stood up then, and Quico spoke to me in Spanish. He said he and Fernando would go along with the women. There was really no trouble in the *colonia*, but this would be better.

I turned and explained to Helen. She looked at the two men, then at Magdalena, and nodded.

I knew the Mexicans would take a few minutes saying good-bye to one another, so I thought I would leave first. I said my good-byes in Spanish and then gave Helen both my hands.

"Don't worry," I said. "These are good people. They're very good friends of mine, and they'll take care of you."

"I can tell."

"And I'll be back in a day or two. Just sit tight."

"All right, Jimmy."

I think it was the first time she called me by my name. I thought she might have been afraid to say it until she heard Magdalena pronounce it a couple of times.

"So long, Helen," I said. "I'll be back before you know it."

I shook hands with Chanate and Nena, then Quico and Fernando.

Quico pointed to his eye and said, "*Nosotros cuidamos,*" which means "We'll keep an eye on things."

I smiled at him and then looked at Fernando, who gave an assuring nod. I had already noticed his quick eyes, but I knew I didn't have to doubt him. These people had a sense of honor, which included not asking indiscreet questions, as they would say, and he would fall right in line. But I also thought that if anyone laid a hand on the American girl, he might well have Fernando to answer to. None of these people were fools. They would help a friend at the same time that they might wish he had taken the matter elsewhere, but of the people gathered, I thought Fernando would see the least taint in the blondie girl.

I gave Helen my hand again, and then I was gone.

On the way back to the line camp, I had plenty to think about. I was glad to have such good friends, and I felt that Magdalena had been as gracious as could be. As I thought about it, I found myself admiring her and wishing I could have spent more time there. I knew Helen was in good hands, and I doubted that Maudenwarlick would find her very soon. And if someone wanted to connect her disappearance with me, I would be back at the line camp, putting in my time with Rudd and Turner.

Whoever this Darcy Melva fellow was, he would be hopping mad. I had gotten the idea that he kept Helen for his own girl whenever he came around, but she seemed to be glad to get away, so I figured he could just get used to it and find someone else. He could try to locate her, but I was sure we had her pretty well stashed until I came up with a plan for both of us to get the hell gone.

Chapter Nine

Things were calm as could be that evening at the boar's nest, but the next morning, not too long after breakfast, we got a surprise visit. We were all sitting around having a second cup of coffee, and no one was in a hurry. Rudd had just lit a cigarette and was sitting back in his chair with his right boot up on the corner of the table. Turner was sitting on the edge of his bunk, barefoot, and was cleaning between his toes by pulling a sock through the crevices. I had taken out my knife and was cleaning my fingernails. Rudd had said we were each going to go out on a separate ride to look around again today, and we were taking our time to get going.

I had lapsed into my own thoughts about how I was going to manage the day. Then all of a sudden I heard hoofbeats as someone came riding into the yard at a trot or a fast walk. Down came Rudd's boot, and his hand was on his gun. Turner paused with his sock halfway through a pull on his right foot as he looked at Rudd. I brushed off the front of my shirt and looked at Rudd also.

"Go see who it is," he said to me.

I got up and stuck my knife in the table, and then on second thought I pulled it loose and put it in the sheath on my hip. With my right hand on the butt of my six-gun, I pulled open the door, and there stood Whitlow.

I thought he had an agitated look on his face as he lifted his chin and pointed at the inside of the shack.

"Is everyone here?"

"Everyone that lives here," I said, standing aside to let him in.

Both Rudd and Turner seemed surprised to see him, but I couldn't be sure of anything with that bunch. Rudd could just as well have told us we were going out on a ride and have known all along that the boss would show up, but from the way he had snapped to at the sound of hoofbeats, I thought the surprise was genuine. Then, as I got a closer look at Whitlow, I noticed he hadn't shaved that morning. That meant he had probably come in a hurry rather than on a plan. I wondered if something had come up, like the law finding out some new information about Jimmy Rooks.

Rudd seemed to have gotten himself smoothed over and was on his feet.

"Coffee?" he asked.

"Sure." Whitlow looked at Turner and then me. "You-all eat breakfast already?"

We both nodded.

"That's good. You-all got plans for the day?"

Turner said "Yeah," and I just moved my head in agreement.

"Good." Whitlow sat in the chair closest to the stove and unbuttoned his coat. Even if he was in a pet about something, he was dressed all the way, with his pistol as well as his vest and watch chain.

Rudd set a cup on the table and poured coffee for the boss. "Anything new?" He sat back down in his chair.

Whitlow scowled and said, "No, nothing at all."

I sat back down to finish my coffee. I had the sense that the boss wanted to talk to Rudd, so I thought I'd hurry up and make myself scarce.

Whitlow looked at me and said, "How about you, Clevis? Have you heard or even thought about anything more that might shed light on what we talked about the other day?"

"You mean Jimmy Rooks and why he might have ended up that way?"

"Yeah, that."

178

I turned down the corners of my mouth and shook my head. "Sure haven't." I knew full well I had just been up to the hilt into something that Jimmy Rooks had at least been interested in, but I didn't think it would do me any good to tell Whitlow. If I had learned anything from him or these other two, it was to keep things under my hat.

"Well," he said, "that's not the only thing in the world. We've got work to do and business to tend to."

"Uh-huh." I tipped up my coffee cup.

"But you know," he went on, "I've thought a little about something you said."

"Oh? What was that?"

"The thing you said about not eating any beef. I thought there was no reason you couldn't." He looked at Rudd. "Not that I came all the way over here to tell you that, you understand, Axel, but I thought it might be a good job for these two boys while you and I looked over some accounts."

"Oh. Uh-huh. Sure." Rudd looked at me and then Turner. "You hear that? You two need to go out and find a beef to kill. Don't get one that's got a brand from anywhere close, you hear?"

I nodded, and Turner did the same.

Rudd brought up his cigarette from where he had been holding it by his side. "Steer or heifer, either one. Bring it all the way back here without puttin' a rope on it, and then, Jimmy, you've got the knife, so you bleed it after Ben shoots it."

That was just like Rudd, to give us orders right down to the last detail. "All right," I said. "Hang it in the lean-to?"

"Yeah."

"Will do." I left Turner to finish with his toes, and I walked outside to get started on the day.

I was coming back from the pasture with a horse on the end of my rope when Turner came out of the shack. "I'll get mine and we'll be ready to go," he said.

When I had come into camp the evening before, I had left my rifle and scabbard strapped onto my saddle. I had noticed Rudd and Turner watching me when I carried the rifle in and out of the shack, so I thought I would give them less to observe. Now as I saddled my horse I was glad I had done it that way. Otherwise, I would probably have left the rifle in the shack rather than go in and get it while Whitlow and Rudd were having a powwow.

Turner didn't waste much time getting his horse ready, and even though I had always seen him as a sloppy sort, he was good with his hands when he was doing a routine job. He wasn't like Rudd, who would shuffle cards for a half hour at a time just to keep his hands limber. He wouldn't have made a good dentist, but he was handy with a gun and a rope and all the gear on a horse.

As he led his horse out and swung aboard, I took a look at him. I hadn't ridden out with anyone else since Jimmy Rooks had died, and now I was partnered up, for the day at least, with Turner. They say a man can be judged by the company he keeps, so I looked at him with the idea that I was seeing what someone else would see, which in turn would reflect on me.

I saw a roughneck who needed a shave and a bath and a change of clothes. His blotchy complexion usually looked dirty anyway, and when he had stubble on his face, which was most of the time, and his floppy hat with the snakeskin hatband, he looked like a perfect specimen of the back-woods coon hunter that he said he was. And even though he seemed to spend most of his time slouching around and spitting tobacco juice, he had a wary eye and a smooth way of moving that suited him for the work he did. Fellows from some trades don't convert too well into cow-punchers — take coal miners or black-smiths, for instance. They're kind of clumsy at things that Turner came by pretty easy, just from the time he had spent around guns and animals.

We rode out onto the rangeland and headed southeast. Turner didn't say much, which was usual for him when there was just the two of us. He seemed to enjoy putting on an intense look as he scanned the countryside, as if he saw more in the landscape than I could. I let him have his game and figured I would just do my job when the time came.

Whenever we saw cattle we rode close enough to read the brands, and since we had made it our business to know about other people's property, we knew at a glance where most of the brands came from.

Finally we saw a steer off by itself, a two-year-old, that wore a brand that was a stranger to us. On the front left shoulder, it carried what looked like a 7M. Turner reined toward the steer and nodded, but when he came within forty yards of it, the animal bolted.

"Let's go ahead and rope it," he called to me.

When I caught up with him, I looked at him and frowned. "Rudd said not to put a rope on anything, just drive it in loose like that."

"Oh, he changed his mind. Before I came out, he told me to go ahead and rope it if we need to."

"Well, why don't we try drivin' it first?"

"That little steer's on his own, and I don't feel like chasin' him stop-and-go all day long. Who knows where he came from or wants to go back to."

It seemed to me like just one more instance of someone changing the plans, so I said, "Let's try it without the rope first."

Turner didn't say anything, just spit out some tobacco juice and pulled down on the front of his hat brim as he spurred his horse. We chased the steer over a couple of low hills, and each time he would do the same thing. He would run way out ahead and stop, and then, when we would come within about fifty or sixty yards of him at a fast walk, he would take off again. Finally Turner reined to a stop, and I did, too.

"What did I tell you?" he said.

"He's jumpy. Why don't we try ridin' way around and then headin' him back in this direction? We're just chasin' him away."

"Jeezechrise, Clevis. How long do you want to spend at this job?"

I shrugged. "Long as it takes, I guess."

"I say we rope him."

I hesitated and then thought, *What the hell.* "I don't care," I said. "Do you want to rope him, or shall I?"

"Why don't you go ahead first?"

"All right," I said, and I untied my rope. I nudged my horse forward at a fast walk, and he knew we were going to rope something.

Turner, who had pulled up on my left, moved forward along with me and a little behind. I thought he would fall back and go around, but he didn't. Usually if two fellows are going to go after a steer, the one that isn't going to rope first will ride on the off side of the animal, usually the right side, so he can haze it toward his partner. But as we moved toward the steer and I started fingering the coils on my rope, I saw that Turner was still sticking close to me on my left. I thought I saw his hand move toward his gun and then away as I turned to see him better. I looked forward to see what the steer was doing, and when I looked around at Turner again, he was drawing his gun.

All in a flash I saw how I was being set

up. I could picture the three of them — Whitlow, Rudd, and Turner — settling on it right after I walked out of the shack. When I thought Turner was cleaning his toes, he was getting instructions on how to kill me. The staging of it came from his own cunning. I could see that, too, in the way that he had stayed on my off side and had waited till I had the rope in my hand and couldn't make a quick move for my gun. And if he shot me while I was roping, it would look as if someone caught me in the act of throwing the wide loop.

I cut my horse sharp around to the left so that he almost collided nose-to-nose with Turner's horse. Mine started a stutter-step, and Turner's started to crow-hop, and then I had a chance. It was hard to shoot when the man with the gun and the target on the other end were both bouncing around, but it was not so hard to rope. I swung my rope once, twice, and three times, and on the third turn of the wrist I threw the rope forward. It was like roping a horse when he wanted to dodge away.

Turner's hat had bounced off in the commotion, and I had his red head as my object. He reached his gun hand up to try to knock the rope aside, but the loop came down around his wrist, and when I pulled my slack, the rope jerked his hand up against his head and sent his six-gun bouncing off the swell of his saddle onto the ground.

My horse dug in as I wrapped my dallies, and as Turner's horse was still sashaying, Turner himself got yanked from the saddle and bounced onto the ground. My horse started pulling backward, but Turner got to his feet and moved with it, coughing and gasping as he pulled on the rope with his left hand and clawed at the noose around his neck with his right.

I knew I had to get to him before he got his gun back in his hands, so I stepped off my horse as if I had a calf to flank. Red-haired Turner was coming at me on the end of the rope, and I could see he had pulled the loop away from his throat and was slipping it up over his jaw. I timed it right and landed a solid punch in the middle of his pink face. I could feel it in my fist. The impact spun him off to the side away from me, but he did manage to flip the rope up and away from his head.

He came at me then, and I realized there wasn't going to be any truce. If I had seen that a second earlier, I could have drawn and fired, but now we were at close quarters.

I tried to punch him again, but my fist skidded off his forehead as he lowered and charged. He got his arms around me, and I knew he wanted to wrestle me to the ground and get his hand on my gun. I sprawled away from him and shoved down with both hands on his head. That pushed him aside, but he came right back at me and tried another bear hug. I locked my right arm down on his left and dropped all my weight onto his upper arm and shoulder. He hit the ground hard, with me on top of him, but he wasn't done.

He reached up with his right hand and sank his fingernails into the back of my left ear, and then he put his thumb against my eye. I smashed him in the nose with the heel of my left hand, and it loosened his grip. He tried to roll me over, but he made it only halfway, and I ended up on top of him with his back on the ground. His right hand was still clawing at me, so I fended it off with my left hand as I pummeled him a couple of times with my right. Then I got both hands on his throat.

He went wild then, bucking and flailing, but I could tell he couldn't concentrate his strength like I was able to do. I already had it over him, and I directed all my strength right down to my hands, where I choked him and slammed him until I felt no resistance. Then, after another long moment, I felt the flesh relax beneath my grip, and I could tell I had killed the man who had tried to kill me.

I got up and stood off to one side, looking down at him. I thought it was too bad for him, the waste of a young life. He shouldn't have tried what he did. He shouldn't have let those others tell him what to do. Then I thought, *No, that wasn't his mistake.* He would do what they told him no matter what. His mistake was in not wanting to kill me as much as I wanted to live. He should have wanted it more, because when it came right down to it, my will was stronger than his until he realized he was fighting for his life, and then it was too late.

It made me wonder if he killed Jimmy Rooks by himself, like he tried to do with me at the beginning, or if he had help. It could have been either way, but I no longer had any doubts as to whether Jimmy's death was an inside or an outside job. They had put a bullet in Jimmy, and I had been on their blacklist from the moment they found out I reported it. And for whatever reason they killed him, they must have figured I knew something about it. But I didn't, even if it had something to do with the girl. I still felt like I was on the outside.

One thing was for sure, though. I was done working for Whitlow and the Kite. Not only that, but before long, someone would be after me.

I looked at Turner again, and I could see bruises on his throat and a rope burn on his neck. To someone who didn't know the details, it might look like vigilante work, and I didn't see any harm in that appearance. But at the same time I was satisfied that in the last minutes of his life, Turner knew the truth. It might have felt like the dark brother all over again, but somewhere as he sank into his pond he would have known it was the *compadre* he tried to double-cross. A man didn't cross this outfit, indeed. I guess I could see who had crossed what. I remembered what I had thought when I found Jimmy Rooks — that he was the wrong man in the wrong place. I didn't have a sense of whether Turner was in the right place, or even if there was a right place for what had just happened, but I did think he was the right man to be where he was.

I looked up and around to find my horse. He was just a little ways off. I needed to get the hell away from here, I thought. So without giving Turner another look or a last good-bye, I went after my horse.

As I rode away, I thought about what I had said a couple of nights earlier, that regardless of how a man died, he deserved a decent burial. I hoped Turner got one, but I didn't think it was my job to see to it. Then I remembered Rudd's sarcastic comments and Turner's opinions on the subject, and I was satisfied that I could leave it to Rudd.

A man didn't cross the outfit, I thought again. No, but he could double-cross anyone that the boss wanted him to turn on. Uh-huh. Then I thought about the part where I was supposed to keep my mouth shut and not go outside with information. Well, that was dandy. I wouldn't tell anyone. I would let someone else find the body and try to determine whether it was a killing or an accident. And meanwhile I was going to get the hell away from Whitlow, the Kite, and anybody connected to it. I had wanted to make my break in an easier way, without any showdowns, but they didn't give me a chance.

I was damn sure done at this outfit, and I had someone waiting for me elsewhere. I was glad I had my rifle and six-gun — and my knife — for all the good they had just done me. But I wanted the rest of my gear, which didn't amount to much but was mine all the same.

I rode back to the vicinity of the line camp and watched it from a distance. I counted the horses in the pasture, figuring in the two that I had taken to Whitlow as well as the two that Turner and I had ridden. There were eleven in the pasture, and I knew them all. One of the horses from Rudd's string was gone, and the horse Whitlow had ridden in on was gone as well. I doubted that they had set a trap for me by having one person ride off with two horses while the other sat inside the shack with a loaded gun. It was more likely that they would assume Turner would get his dirty work done.

I watched the shack for a good half hour and saw no movement. Then I decided I had better go ahead and make a quick grab of things before anyone came back to wait on Turner's report. So I rode on into the camp at a trot, swung down, and went to the door. I pushed it open and sank back, half expecting to hear the roar of gunfire.

But I met with nothing. The boar's nest was still and quiet. Just a few hours earlier, three men had sat here and made light of my life while I was out roping a horse. Well, things were changed, I thought. I made quick work of gathering up my bedroll and warbag, and before I stepped outside I took a last look around. I was sure I wouldn't be back, come what may. It took me less than a minute to clear out my stuff and a little more than a minute to tie it onto the back of my saddle. It occurred to me that I was riding off on a company horse, but I figured that would be the least of their reasons for wanting to find me. I made fast tracks away from the line camp, looking back only once to see the shack recede in the distance as my horse kicked up dust. I thought the fat was in the fire now, but at least I knew where I stood. And I was glad to be getting away from Whitlow, Rudd, and the Kite.

Chapter Ten

As I rode along, I got to thinking about what a nice fire the line camp would have made and how much more interesting it would have been to look back at if it had been going up in flames. But it was just as well I didn't. For one thing, it wasn't mine to set a match to, and I had decided I was pretty well through with making free with other people's property. For another thing, I didn't need to give Whitlow and Rudd yet one more reason to try to hunt me down.

My thoughts went back and forth from one subject to another, and I couldn't come up with a full explanation of why they had Turner try to do me in. I knew it had something to do with Jimmy Rooks, but whatever he had done was lost to me. Yet it seemed they thought I was in on it. I couldn't make it out. The only other thing I could come up with was that he and I had seen the same girl. But that seemed pretty thin. Whoever Darcy Melva was, I couldn't imagine him getting someone like Whitlow to snuff out his own men like so many candles. From what Helen said, the man was a blackmailer, but he would have to have something pretty big on Whitlow to get him to do another man's rat-killing. I had to imagine Melva way higher on the ladder than Whitlow, and then I had to imagine Whitlow being guilty of something a lot bigger than the things Tome had mentioned. I just didn't know enough to make it fit.

I did know two things. One was that someone had just tried to kill me and hadn't quite made it, and the other was that I was going to get to see that walloping girl again, and sooner than I had expected. So with one force pushing me and the other pulling me, I made pretty good time on the borrowed horse.

As I got to thinking about Helen and where I would go to see her, I thought of Magdalena as well. If I was excited about seeing Helen in one way, I was glad in another way that I was going to see Nena. I didn't know if I was anywhere close to the mark, but it seemed as if the scene the evening before had brought us closer together. Maybe she didn't feel anything, but I did. It was as if her abetting me amounted to some kind of a recognition of what I had done with Helen; and to me, at least, Magdalena's knowing that about me dispelled some of the fear I had of her being so much more of a woman than I was a man. That was an interesting thought, whether I was right or not. And in one corner of it was the knowledge that I was on my way to see both of them now.

As I imagined walking into Nena's house and seeing the two of them, I tried to picture what I would look like to them. I knew I was a bit smudged and scuffed from my fight with Turner, and I thought it wouldn't hurt if I stopped at the river and cleaned up. With that idea I stopped at the crossing, which had good gravelly shoals where a fellow could crouch to wash himself.

With that job done, I felt clean and presentable in spite of my clothes having more dirt and dust than I could beat out of them. Back on my way to Mexican town, and still keeping to the south side of the river, I got to thinking about how much I should tell to this person or that. I had just killed a man — fair and square, for all that, but I had done it nevertheless — and if I took some grim satisfaction in not telling anyone in authority, I needed to think how close to my chest I wanted to play things with these other people.

I tried to put things in sequence. What I

wanted to do was to take Helen and make a run for it. I had with me what little money I had put away, and I could get a horse from Chanate or someone else in the *colonia*. I might even buy two, and I could leave the Kite horse to be sent back to Whitlow. If Helen was willing to go, I would probably be wise not to tell her about the fight with Turner until we were long gone. Otherwise it might scare her into not going.

Then, if it looked like we were hitting the trail, I could decide how much to tell Chanate or Nena. I thought that as long as I didn't lie to them, I would be all right in my own conscience if I didn't tell them everything. And if I was going far away with Helen, I might not see them again for a long time, if ever, and leaving out a detail or two wouldn't stand between us. That might be the best, I thought, to play it close until I saw how things were going to shake out.

With my plan pretty well formed for the time being, I rode into Mexican town at about noon or a little after. The smell of woodsmoke reminded me that within the walls of many of the houses, dark-haired women were patting out tortillas, stirring food as it bubbled in clay pots, or turning meat as it sputtered in iron skillets. In one of those houses I had the prospect of seeing two girls, one dark and one light — and, I hoped, both smiling. The day was starting to shape up much better than it had been a few fours earlier, when I was climbing back onto my horse and coiling up my rope.

My outlook started to change, though, when I stopped at Magdalena's house and found no one there. I knocked and got no answer, then knocked again, and again, without hearing a sound from inside. I told myself they might have gone to Chanate and Clementina's, so I mounted up and rode that way.

The doorbell tinkled as I went into the butcher shop. Everything seemed in order there, with hams and sides of bacon and chains of sausages hanging on the back wall, and the air rich as always with the smell of garlic and animal fat. Chanate had a shoulder of beef on his wooden block and was boning it with a thin-bladed knife. When he saw me, he stuck the knife in the block and came out from behind the counter, wiping his hands on his apron. He smiled as we shook hands.

"Hello, Yimi. How does it go?"

"Pretty well. And yourself?"

"Oh, very well, thanks to God."

"And Tina?"

"She's fine also."

"And your niece?"

"Rosa Linda? She's fine, too."

"That's good. And Nena? Is she around here?"

His smile faded. "I don't know where she is."

"Oh," I said. "I passed by her house, but I didn't find anyone there."

"Oh, maybe she went someplace. She was here a little while ago, but I don't know where she would have gone."

"Well, that's all right. Was the American girl with her? I was wondering if she was all right."

"The light-colored girl? Oh, Yimi, she went away already."

I felt everything drop. "She did? When?"

"Last night. I think she was with Nena barely two hours. That's what Nena said."

"Did she leave with someone, or did somebody come for her?"

Chanate shook his head. "No, Yimi. She decided to go herself. She left walking."

I felt as if I had a rock in the pit of my stomach. After all my trouble, she had gone back of her own accord. I shook my head. "I need to talk to Nena, to find out what the girl said."

Chanate patted me on the shoulder. "Don't worry too much, Yimi. If she doesn't want to be here, it's better that she goes."

"But they have her in something like a jail. That's why I wanted to get her out."

Chanate raised his eyebrows. "The door must be open, if she can walk back in."

I could feel myself on edge, all over again. "I've got to do something about it."

He shrugged. "For right now, maybe there's not much you can do."

I went back to my earlier idea. "I need to talk to Nena. Do you know where she is, or when she'll be back?"

"Oh, you know, she comes and goes. You can wait here a little while, and pretty soon it will be time to eat. Stay here at least that long."

"I don't know. I need to find out what the blond girl said. I need to know if she went back because she wanted to or because she was afraid."

He shook his head. "I don't know."

"Nena can tell me something. Did she say the girl was afraid?"

"She didn't say anything."

"Was she worried?"

"No, not really."

"Well, I need to do something."

"Wait awhile, Yimi. Calm down a little." He patted me on the shoulder again. "Pretty soon we'll eat."

I heaved a sigh. "Oh, all right. I'll wait." Food always sounded good to me, but at the moment it wasn't as high on the list as it should have been.

Chanate went back to boning the shoulder of beef as I slouched against the meat case and watched him. He asked how things were going at the ranch, and I told him not very good, that I thought I was going to quit my job and find a better place to work. He nodded without looking up. I had the impression that he thought it would be a good change but he didn't want to say anything that would reflect on the way I had been making a living.

We talked on, making conversation about small things. He told me how he started out working as a small boy, throwing stones at the crows when they came to the cornfield. From there he learned to watch sheep and goats, and then he got a chance to go to work at slaughtering. *La matanza,* he called it. For several years he scalded and scraped hogs, along with the regular killing and skinning. Then he ended up with his butcher shop, *la carnicería,* where he was happy, thanks to God, and had a good wife, and they lived *tranquilo.*

He made it all sound so clean and honest that it made me wonder if some of the rest of us were more cut out for trouble to begin with. I wondered if it was because a person was restless by nature, or wanted more excitement in life, or just had something in his blood that kept him from leading a calm, safe existence. I didn't know. I could imagine Chanate's nephew, Quico, headed in the direction of a steady life. But not all Mexicans were like that, not any more than all whites were one way or the other. I had known Mexicans who, if they did not live in the midst of trouble, at least had some of it in their blood. Now that I thought of it, Nena might be that way herself. I had heard her say she was the black sheep, *la oveja negra,* and I could remember thinking that she was my kind of person. At that time I had seen myself as living on the edge of trouble. Then, with this business with Jimmy Rooks, I had been pushed into the middle. I wanted to get back to the edge, and I didn't like the way I was feeling at the moment. I wished to hell Nena would show up so I could talk to her and try to make sense of what happened with Helen.

But time dragged on. I watched as Chanate finished boning the meat and then trimmed off the biggest gobs of fat. After that he whittled all the odd pieces into what I would call stew meat, though I'm not sure what he would call them, and he sliced the larger pieces into thin steaks. As he was putting the last bits into the meat case, a person appeared at the doorway in back. It was Rosa Linda, who addressed him as *tío* and told him dinner was ready.

At his invitation I went with him to the back of the house, where Rosa Linda was setting another plate on the table. As I got closer I saw only two places set. Both plates had food served on them. From that I imagined that the women would eat later. I knew it was normal in a house such as this one for people to eat at different times, yet I wondered if Clementina was keeping her niece away from this questionable *gringo*. If she was, I couldn't blame her. Then I figured out that there had been only one place set before I showed up, so the women had already decided to eat later. I realized the arrangement might have had more to do with me if Rosa Linda had been taking away a third plate rather than setting a second. That thought cheered me up, so I took my seat at the table and didn't worry.

Rosa Linda brought a stack of tortillas wrapped in a towel. I could smell them. They were warm corn tortillas. She set them on the table between her uncle and me. I thanked her, and she glided out of my sight. Then I turned and saw that she had sat in a wooden rocking chair at the edge of the dining area.

The food had a welcome taste. I had missed out on a meal the last two times I had been in the *colonia,* and now I relished the tortillas, meat, and beans. I took the meat to be lamb or mutton. I had noticed in households like this, years earlier, that people did not often ask what kind of meat they were eating. But it was a point of interest with me, and since Chanate was a butcher, I confirmed it with him.

"*¿Borrego?*"

"*Sí, borrego.*"

At the edge of my field of vision I could see the pale pink of Rosa Linda's dress. I turned to glance at her again, and she gave me a kind of smile, as she might to any of her uncle's friends who came to eat. She looked so pure and untainted that I felt guilty for stealing a glance. Then I had a funny thought. I remembered a superstition that some of them had, that a person should not eat in front of a pregnant woman without offering her food. Otherwise, the baby would be born with its mouth open, and it would wander through life that way, looking for food. There had been times when I had been eating and had been tempted to ask a woman, just for a joke, whether she was pregnant. Now, as I sat at Chanate's table beneath the Last Supper, the joke went through my mind. It was so far from being probable that I shook my head. After chastising myself for a moment for even thinking of such a joke, I found myself feeling happy that such a clean, innocent person lived in the same world as I did. For as much as I cringed at the thought of what kind of a person I had been, at least I was doing something about it. That thought helped me feel like less of a hypocrite sitting and eating in the presence of decent people.

I looked up at the Last Supper, and those fellows weren't scowling at anything either. They might have been having lamb, too, and good goblets of wine. I thought of a joke I had heard about that scene. In addition to learning from the Mexicans how to pray, I had heard at least three jokes about the Last Supper. The one I thought of now was the one that said, everyone who wants to look good in the picture needs to get on this side of the table. Maybe it was irreverent, but it wasn't mean, and it took nothing away from my sense that I was under the roof of good people and eating their food. I was thankful, and I was happy.

It didn't last forever, though. One thing about eating in shifts is that people don't sit around and gab for an hour after the meal. They get up and make room for someone else. When Chanate was done, he waited for me to finish, and then he pushed back his chair and said he was going back to the shop. I took leave of the women, thanked God for the food, and went out front with Chanate. He said he was going to go see a *señora* who raised chickens, and he asked if I would like to go along. I said no, I would go see if Nena was home and then I would go to the other side of the river to see what I could learn about the girl. He wished me well and I left the shop, with the doorbell tinkling as I heard the echo of his words, *Que te vaya bien.*

Getting no answer for the second time at Magdalena's house, I was feeling anxious again. I needed to find out what had really happened with Helen, and I didn't have forever. Before long, if it hadn't happened already, Rudd would find out what had become of Turner, and I was going to have to make myself scarce. Whoever came after me would probably look for me first in town, so I needed to take care of my business there and then decide what to do next.

I crossed the bridge into the main part of Monetta, such as it was, and still didn't have a good idea as to how I was going to get in touch with Helen. It was too early in the day for Iris to be pitching her mop water, and I didn't think I would have any luck trying to get through the front door. I imagined Maudenwarlick would be even more on their guard after the girl had been gone for a stretch of time the night before, but of course I had no way of knowing what they knew. In spite of all my hesitations, I could not keep myself from riding past the boardinghouse.

First I rode down the street that went past the front door. The place was up ahead on my right, and as I came closer I could not see any movement. Passing it, I saw that the front door was closed and the sitting room was vacant, neither of which surprised me. I thought everyone might be still sitting at the dinner table, but for all I knew, Maudenwarlick could have herded the girls back to their rooms and were locking them up, one by one, to keep out the wolf. It seemed to me that Iris the *enanita* did her sweeping and mopping between the dinner hour and the supper hour, but I didn't want to be riding back and forth in the hopes of catching her out front. Still, I didn't want to wait in back all afternoon, either, especially if anyone was on the lookout. I kept tossing things back and forth with myself, and the anxiety was eating me up. I had to know how things stood with this girl, and I didn't have much time to do it.

I rode around the block and came up the alleyway that ran past the back of the house and lot. I thought, all I needed was for Iris to appear, but that was like waiting on a hunting stand and hoping for a deer to show. Wishing didn't make it happen. Still I said to myself, *Iris, Iris, dear little* enanita, *please come tripping out with a thunder mug or a douche bucket, and carry a message back for me. Please, please.* But no one appeared. The backyard remained blank.

I got down from my horse and waited for

ten minutes, fifteen, until the back door opened. My heartbeat picked up. Out stepped a little person, the *enanita* in her blond curls and long dress. She was on her way to the outhouse with a bucket, sure enough, tilting forward in the funny way that she walked, and leaning to her left to counterbalance the weight of the pail. Then the outhouse closed her from view. I heard the hinges on the door and then a splash inside.

I moved forward between the outhouse and the shed, and as she stepped back onto the path, I whistled.

She turned and looked at me without showing any surprise.

"Iris," I said in a loud whisper, "come here."

She set down the bucket and walked toward me. "What do you want?"

"Iris, you have to help me. You're my only friend in this."

"What do you want?"

"I need to know, is Helen still here?"

"Of course she is."

"Is she in trouble?"

"I don't know."

"Will she come and talk to me?"

"I don't know that either."

"Will you ask her?"

"I'm busy right now. I'm cleaning the rooms."

"Would you please go ask her? Please, Iris. You've been nothing but good to me, and I've tried to be good to you."

"I don't know."

"Oh, come on, Iris. Please." I felt like offering her a dollar, but I thought it might be overdoing things.

"I don't know. I'm busy. But I have to come back out again in a few minutes."

All this time, she had not looked me in the face, so I had been looking down on her head of tight little curls, pale in the sunlight. Now she raised her head and gave me a blank look, then turned, went back to her tin bucket, picked it up, and scurried back to the house.

Sure enough, she was back in less than ten minutes, leaning and straining on another pail of slop. I felt I should have helped, but I didn't want to do anything that would be interfering or crossing a line. When she had finished dumping the bucket, I stepped into view again.

"What do you think?" I asked.

"Wait till I go inside, and then go to the back door. She'll talk to you there."

I felt a stab of worry. "Why can't she come out?"

"I don't know. She just said she would talk to you there."

I tried to think of what to say next, but the *enanita* just turned and hurried away. She had not even set down her bucket this time, so I could see she didn't want to dilly-dally. I watched her go up the steps and in through the door, and then I went on a fast walk to the back steps.

I thought it could be a trap. It was the same feeling I had had earlier when I went to clear out of the boar's nest. But again, nothing happened to harm me. I went up the steps and paused at the door.

It opened a crack, and I could see Helen's blond hair.

"Helen, are you all right?"

"Yes," she whispered.

"Why did you come back to this place?"

"I had to."

"Did you want to?"

"I had to."

"I don't understand." I could feel the tension flowing from her to me, so I took a breath and tried to calm myself. "What about us?"

"I don't know."

"Listen, Helen. This isn't making any sense. Why don't you just come out and we can talk for a while? Just five minutes."

"I can't. I'm sorry, but I can't see you now."

"You mean you can't, physically? Does someone have a chain on you?"

"No. I just can't do anything right now, all right?"

"Why?"

"I just can't." She sounded as if she was on the verge of crying.

"Are you afraid of something? Of me?"

"No, not of you."

"But you can't see me?"

"No."

"Do you want me to go away?"

"I guess you have to, if I can't see you."

"I mean, do you want me to go away for good?"

She didn't answer.

"Do you want me to come back?"

This time she waited ten or fifteen seconds until she answered. "Yes, I think so. I would like that."

The door closed, and I hurried away in a daze. Back at my horse, as I checked my cinch, I saw that my hands were shaking. I made myself take deep breaths and calm down. I told myself it was just a girl, but at the same time I knew she had me hooked. It was even more than that. It was as if we had had one of those blood ceremonies I'd heard about, where two people each opened a vein and held their wrists together. Whatever was in her blood was in mine. That was how it felt. I had been inside of her, in actuality, and I had taken possession of her. Or so I thought. But now it was working both ways. Whatever had a hold of her was doing the same to me, or she was passing it on to me. If I had had her for a little while, I didn't now. Something else had her, and she had me. That was more like it. She was vein-to-vein with me on one wrist, and she was the same way with someone else on the other side. I knew his name — Darcy Melva — but I couldn't see his face. Like before, all I could see was his hand.

Chapter Eleven

Riding back out onto the main street, I felt that I needed a drink. The visit with Helen had wrung me out in short order, I thought, until I realized it had been a buildup of a few things — the fight with Turner, the disappointment of finding her gone, the tension of waiting to find out if I could see her, and then the frustration of not being able to see any more of her than I did. It was no wonder I needed a drink, or at least felt I did.

Then I got to thinking, this Darcy Melva had a hold on Helen like drink had a hold on some people. I didn't think it had that strong a hold on me yet, but I knew I had a weakness for it. And I think that helped me understand the weakness she had. Not only did I feel a strong pull toward her, but I also felt sympathy. I knew she had been shaken by what had happened, and I wanted to be the one who made her feel better. Of course, I wanted to be with her again, plain and simple, but I also wanted to rescue her from her misery.

But neither of those things was going to happen right now. I was going to go have a

213

drink, even as I realized I might have a weakness for it. I told myself I just needed to be careful.

If there was anything good about my short visit with Helen, it was that I hadn't lost much time. Somewhere out there, Rudd was either wondering about Turner or taking a course of action after finding him. I didn't think anyone would come for me in the Jack-Deuce, but Rudd or others would look for me there and follow me. So I was just going to nip in there, as I had heard an Englishman say, and be on my way again. As to where I was going to go, I hadn't planned that far ahead yet. The smartest thing would be to run like hell, to get as far away from Monetta, Jimmy Rooks, and Helen as I could get. But if I was going to do that, I wouldn't be stopping at the Jack-Deuce. So even if I didn't know for sure what I was going to do, I knew what I wasn't doing at the moment. I wasn't running like a wise man. I was doing something Rudd made fun of me for. I was thinking — and worse, I was thinking about how I was going to get that girl out of the house. I remembered riding away and wondering which window was hers. It was probably on the upper floor, I thought, or she wouldn't have had to come to the door to talk to me.

She had sounded so hopeless that it made me sad to think of her all shut up in that house. I asked myself why she had gone back. An action like that didn't show any more brains than a sheep has. It had to be some kind of power or some type of bond. I could remember stories about white people who were captured by Indians, then tormented and turned into mindless things. When other whites would find them, they would act as if they didn't remember a thing about their earlier lives. Maybe they didn't, or maybe they were afraid to. They would cling to the Comanches or Kiowas who had done such savage things to them, and if they were rescued by the whites, they would go like livestock home to their masters. I didn't think Helen was that far gone, to have had her earlier mind wiped out, but she did go back to the people who held her by force.

I tried to clear my head of these things for a moment as I got down from my horse and tied him up in front of the Jack-Deuce. Reminding myself that I needed to keep my wits about me, I took a long look all around, touched the handle on my six-gun, and went inside.

Sure enough, Tome and Goings were sitting at a table. I called for a glass of beer and carried it over to sit with them.

"You must have an easy life," said Tome. "I see you in here almost as often as I am."

"I work hard for the privilege," I said as I nodded to Goings and sat down. I took a long drink on my beer.

"That's good to know." Tome adjusted his spectacles. "Any news?"

"Oh, maybe. I got to see that girl again."

"The one that Maud has under her wing?"

"Yes, that one."

"Well, what did you find out?"

"I don't know." I looked at him, and he seemed interested, so I went on. "I talked her into gettin' away from there, and I went and stashed her with the Mexicans — with Chanate's niece, Magdalena."

"Oh, now there's a good one. You should have left the white girl where she was and gone by yourself."

"Sometimes I think so. But I didn't. Then, when I came back the next day, which was today, I found out the girl had gone back to the boardinghouse."

"That's no good."

"No, it sure isn't. They keep her like a prisoner, and she goes back to them."

Tome shook his head.

"The thing is," I went on, "I think there's someone behind it all. I think they keep her for their boss. Wait, that didn't sound right. They work for a man, and they do whatever he says. And I think he's the one that keeps her there, through them."

"That doesn't sound good at all. I wonder why you're even bothering with her. But then again, if you got her away from there, maybe I can figure it out."

I turned down the corners of my mouth and nodded each way. "If it was just a matter of her liking him better, that would be one thing. But I think she went back just because she was afraid."

Tome sipped on his drink, as if he was giving it some consideration. "Sounds like this girl has some flaws, and you'd be better off leaving it alone, but maybe you've crossed the Rubicon with her."

"What's that mean?"

"Crossing the Rubicon. It's an old phrase. It means doing something you can't take back."

"Oh, uh-huh."

"In other words, maybe you're in too deep and can't pull out." He looked at Goings, who had been silent all this time, and he said, "In a manner of speaking."

Then he looked back at me. "What's the fella's name?"

I looked around at the shadows and then said, in a low voice, "Darcy Melva."

"Never heard of him. Don't know a thing about him. Is he just another whore-master, or is he some kind of a kingpin?"

"Probably more of the latter. I gather he's got some property, so I'd guess he's got businesses elsewhere."

"Well, it sounds sticky. Don't you have anything better to do with yourself?"

I laughed a short, nervous laugh and took another drink of my beer. There was all this business about Turner and Jimmy Rooks, but I didn't want to open it up at the moment. "I guess not," I said. Then I turned to Goings. "I'll tell you, though, I thought of something you could do for me, and I'd pay you for it."

He gave me a calm smile. "What's that? Do away with the linchpin?"

Tome laughed. "I think Jimmy here is the linchpin, but that's all right."

"Well," I said, "it would be handy, but since we don't know anything about him or where he keeps himself, maybe we'll wait on that. What I've got in mind is something simpler."

"Go ahead."

"I thought you might be able to get in the front door of the boardinghouse and take a look around. Then, when I see you next, you could give me an idea of the layout of the place. I think that if I ever end up inside, I'd like to know ahead of time how it's laid out."

Goings raised his eyebrows. "Just walk in and snoop around?"

"Well, I think you could say you're looking for work. Just pick a time when there's no one in front — there's a kind of lobby or sitting room there — and go inside. You ought to be able to get a look around by the time someone asks you what you're doing there."

"And then they throw me out."

I shrugged. "I think you can act the part, and no one'll do anything rough to you. Not that anyone could anyway, except for Warlick maybe, and I think he's got more bark than bite."

"I don't know. I guess I could try it."

"What would you think of a dollar for the job?" I had about a third of a glass of beer left, and I drank half of that as I waited for his answer.

"Sounds good enough."

Tome laid his pipe on the table. "And who knows? You might be able to get a look at the midget while you're there."

I brought out a silver dollar and laid it on the table in front of Goings. "There it is," I said. "However much you can do, I'll appreciate it." Then, looking from him to Tome, I said, "I hate to rush my drink, but I need to be on my way." I downed the last of my beer.

Tome pursed his lips. "Not going back to work, I hope."

"No, I think I'll go hide from it."

"Good idea."

As I walked out of the Jack-Deuce, I realized I had avoided telling Tome a couple of things — why I was going to hide, and that I was going to try to see Magdalena before I left town.

Once outside, I looked up and down the street and saw no one to worry about. A man and a woman were walking with their backs to me on the east side of the street, and a couple of loafers sat in the shade on the west side. Looking up at the sun, I thought it might be late enough in the day for someone to be on my trail. I stood close to my horse as I tightened the cinch, and then after another casual look around, I slipped my knife and sheath off my belt and into my left boot. Then I mounted up and rode toward Mexican town.

I was glad to get across the bridge, and I was gladder yet to get an answer when I knocked on Magdalena's door. She opened it a crack and then pulled it open the rest of the way.

"Yimi. How good that you came. Come on in."

I looked over my shoulder. "What do you think if I put my horse in back first?"

A serious look came over her face. "Sure. I'll wait for you here."

I took the horse around back and tied him to a clothesline pole, then went around the little house and met Nena again at the front door. She invited me in, and I stood in her living room with my hat in my hands.

"Well, how are you, Yimi? How has it gone for you? My uncle said you passed by his house and you were worried."

"Yes, I am worried. You know, I don't understand why the girl left. But I think she was afraid. What did it seem like to you?"

"Maybe so. She just said she had to go back, and she went away on foot."

I shook my head. "I don't know what to do."

"Can you talk to her?"

"I went by there, and I was able to talk

for a few minutes, but no more." I looked at Nena and took in the dark hair, the rich color of her skin, the clear expression in her eyes. At that moment I wished I wasn't hooked by the blondie girl, but I was.

"What are you going to do, then?"

"I don't know. What did you think of her, Nena? Tell me."

She widened her eyes. "Well, I thought she was very nice. But if she doesn't want to stay with you, then maybe she will cause you trouble. She will put stones in your road without even wanting to."

"Up until now it's been more worry than trouble."

"But if you're hiding your horse in back of my house, well, what then? Yimi, I can tell you are worried about more than whether she loves you."

I glanced at the door and back at Nena. "Actually, my bigger trouble is about something else."

Her face was soft but attentive. "Something else?"

"Yes. You remember the story about my partner? The one who was killed. Well, they tried to do something like that to me."

She took in a sharp breath. "Yimi! Did they shoot at you?"

"It was just one, another *compañero*, and

I didn't give him the chance to shoot. I was lucky."

"So you think the others will come for you?"

"Maybe."

"Then what are you going to do?"

"I was thinking I might go to the sheep camp to stay with Quico and Fernando for one night. What do you think of that?"

She nodded. "And then?"

"I have to decide if I want to wait for this girl or just go away. I think she wants me, but she's afraid. If I can convince her to leave again, we won't stop."

"Do what you think is best, Yimi."

"Do you think I should just leave?"

"I can't say. You know better how you feel."

I looked at her for a moment without speaking. I had a pretty good idea of what she really thought, and I admired her for not saying anything that might offend me. Then I said, "Nena, I think I'd better go." There I was again, in a hurry to leave.

"To the sheep camp?"

"Yes."

"If you have to go, I think that's a good place. Look, we can go out the back door."

"All right." I followed her to the door, where she opened it and stood aside as I walked through. Then she stepped outside with me and closed the door behind her.

"I hope everything goes well for you," she said. "I hope you have a good journey and arrive safe at the sheep camp."

"Thank you, Nena, and thank you for your help with the girl." I gave her my hand, then turned to my horse as I put on my hat.

At that moment, Rudd stepped into view from around the corner of the house. I took him in all at a glance, from his narrow-brimmed black hat and thin mustache to his tight buttoned vest on down to his stovepipe boots. He was holding a gun leveled at me.

"Move slow, Clevis," he said. "I don't want to have to put a hole in you right here."

"You'd rather do it somewhere else."

"Let's not worry about more than one thing at a time. Hold your right hand up, and take off your gunbelt with your left. Lay it on the ground off to the side."

I did as I was told.

"Now, sit down and take off your boots. And stay away from that gun." He had told me to move slow, but he wasn't wasting any time.

"This is more trouble than you went to

with Jimmy Rooks," I said, thinking I might slow things down.

"Let's not worry about him either."

"Someone did, or they wouldn't have done him in."

"He crossed the boss. That's what happens to people who do that."

It didn't make enough sense. The only thing Jimmy and I had done to Whitlow was talk about getting free, and as far as I knew, Jimmy hadn't done as much as I had done to go outside the gang. "I don't think he did," I said.

"It doesn't matter what you think. Shut up and sit down."

I lowered myself to the ground.

"Now take off your boots and shake 'em out."

I knew he was doing this to flush out any knife or hideout gun I might have, and I saw a smug look cross his face as the knife rattled out onto the ground. It lay at my ankles, almost within my reach.

"Now scoot back," he said.

I moved backward a couple of feet and leaned back with my hands on the ground.

Rudd waved the gun at Nena, who stood to my right and back a ways. "Now you, *chiquita*. Pick up that gunbelt and bring it over to me. The belt."

It sounded strange to hear someone speaking English to her, but I knew she understood it. As she crossed in front of me, I wondered how much of our Spanish he had heard and understood. But if I said anything more to her in Spanish, it would just rile him. So I kept quiet as she leaned over and picked up the gunbelt.

"Now," he said, "stay off to one side as you bring it to me."

I think she had the idea already, as she had been careful to step over the knife. Now, as she picked up the belt and holster, she straightened up and stood between Rudd and me.

"Get out of the way," he said. "Over there. Don't think I won't shoot a woman, especially a Mexican. I said, move!"

She had given just enough of a distraction for me to push forward and lay my hand on the knife handle. As she stepped aside, I gave my best throw and stuck the knife right below the top button of Rudd's vest.

Magdalena was cool as could be. She took a couple of more steps to the left and pulled the pistol out of the holster.

Rudd, meanwhile, had a look of great surprise on his face, and then he bent forward and seemed absorbed at looking at the knife in his abdomen. He lowered his right hand to his side, with the gun pointing downward. He held his left hand against his vest, with two fingers on each side of the blade as the blood welled out. He seemed like a man all by himself in a world far away.

I was crouched on all fours now, ready to move one way or another, depending on what he did. I made a little "ch-ch" sound to Nena, and she tossed me the gun. I caught it and waited, hoping not to have to touch off a shot here in the *colonia*.

I kept my eye on Rudd's pistol hand as he lifted his head from studying the knife in his stomach. He raised the gun to shooting level and kept going up with it, as if he was in a trance. It reminded me of a fellow I had seen once in a tavern. He was having some kind of a fit — apoplectic, or something like that — and he raised his beer glass up over his right shoulder, all in slow motion, and flung the glass behind him just before he fell over backward. That was the way Rudd looked as he stood up straight and his eyes rolled up toward his eyebrows. Then, instead of falling over backward, he slumped and fell to his left as the six-gun bounced off his right shoulder and hit the ground.

I rose up and stepped forward, covering him with my gun. His mouth was moving and his right boot was twitching, but I could tell he was done for.

Nena stood at my left as she spoke. "Who is he?"

"His name is Rudd. Axel Rudd. He's one of the other two who worked at the ranch."

"And they killed your partner?"

"I'm convinced of it now. But I'm not sure why." I looked at the knife handle and the upper part of the blade, and I saw that blood was still trickling out of the wound. "He thought I was stupid. Maybe I am, but I wasn't as sure of myself as he was."

She handed me the gunbelt. "What are you going to do now?"

"Well, I imagine the first thing to do is to get him away from here. I'll find his horse, and as soon as it's dark, I'll take him somewhere. Maybe to the crossing, where they left my friend." I looked at her as I buckled on the belt.

"And after that?"

"I don't know. I guess I'll go to the sheep camp like I said."

"Are you going to go away, or are you going to wait for the girl?"

"I'm not sure. I need to think about it a little more, but I would feel guilty if I left her with things the way they are."

Magdalena's dark hair was shining in the sun as she said, "I don't think anyone would blame you if you went away."

I gathered she meant anyone in her family. "I know," I said, "but I feel that I haven't finished here yet." I raised my eyebrows and looked at her. "You think I should be."

"You know, Yimi, I like the girl and she is very nice, but I think she is missing something. I don't know if she is worth it. You put yourself in the mouth of the wolf."

I pointed at Rudd. "I think I'm in more trouble here than I am with her."

"You don't think this one has anything to do with her?"

"I don't know. I've thought about it, but I can't see how. I can't see it at all."

"Well, you know someone has his foot on her neck, and she might be part of the reason this man Rudd came after you."

"I know. And if there's a connection, it would be better for me to know it before I go away. That is to say, if I go."

She nodded and smiled as she repeated what she had said earlier. "You do what you think is best."

I smiled back. "Thanks. For right now, that means getting rid of this fellow and going to the sheep camp. I have a little bit of time, because it will take the big boss a while to find out what happened and to decide what to do next." I used the word *patrón* to mean the big boss, and she used it when she spoke back.

"The big boss, he's crooked, isn't he?"

"Yes."

"Well, it's good to get away from crooked people."

"Do you mean the girl, too?"

"I don't say that, Yimi. You know the best how you feel."

Yes, I did. I felt stupid. If I was smart I would just leave, and if I had any courage, I would ask Nena to go with me. The worst that could happen would be for her to say no. And she might. She knew I was stuck on the blondie girl, and she knew, as I did, that I wasn't finished here yet. But I sure wasn't going to forget how cool she was when Rudd had the drop on us.

Chapter Twelve

When I left Rudd's body at the crossing, I felt there was some fairness in dumping him off the way they had done to Jimmy Rooks. Just as I had felt with Turner, I wasn't sure that the right man was in the right place, but it seemed as if things were getting closer to being that way. Rudd was the right man to be tied over a saddle, given what he had in mind for me, and the place where I left him was at least fitting. I doubted he would stay there very long, but once again I thought I would go on my own way and let someone else find him. Killing a man wasn't all that cheerful and light a thing to do, but once it was done, and when it was justified like this, I wasn't going to wallow in afterthoughts. I had to look out for myself. Twice now, I had had someone come after me, and I would be a fool to think Whitlow was going to leave things go and not try to settle the score.

This idea of whether the right man was in the right place was not based on anything factual, as much as it was a way of trying to nail down a broader idea or notion that things didn't make sense. Try as I might, I couldn't make things fit or connect. I had even less doubt than before that Whitlow's men killed Jimmy Rooks, but I couldn't figure out why. Rudd said Jimmy had crossed the boss, and I had no idea of how he might have done it directly. And if it had something to do with Helen, I couldn't see where it was crossing Whitlow. Nor could I imagine how Melva could get Whitlow to rub out both Jimmy and me.

I had it pictured as if it was a diamond or some figure like that, taller than it was wide. Jimmy was at the bottom point. He went up and to the right, where he tried to do something with the girl. From there it went up and to the left, to the top point, where this fellow Melva had smoke pouring out of him, he was so mad. From there it went down and to the left to Whitlow, who sent orders down the ladder to punish Jimmy. If I put myself in Jimmy's spot, it worked the same way, up and around the diamond. Nena could see it, too, in simpler form — I tried to steal away with a girl, and two thugs came after me. It made sense, except for the part about Melva getting Whitlow to make the move. I didn't know enough to connect that side of the diamond.

I did know one thing, though. I had underestimated both Melva and Whitlow. I had brushed off Melva as someone who had a name like a weed, but he was deep enough to have a leech-hold on the girl, and he might well have had the power to get someone to do his killing. I had smirked at Whitlow for stealing sheep, and I had seen him as a stuffed-shirt bully who liked to practice his glare. Maybe he was all of that, and maybe he was under Melva's thumb in ways I couldn't make out, but on his own he was still deadly as a snake. I had him to worry about first and foremost. I needed to be on the lookout for Melva, too, and since I didn't know what he looked like or how he played in, or even where he lived, I needed to be alert for anything that even looked like a shadow of a threat.

I had plenty to think about, then, as I rode across country in the dark on my way to the sheep camp. When I got there I saw a faint light in the window, so at least I wasn't waking up anybody. As I came closer to the cabin, the front door opened. Quico called out in Spanish to ask who went there. When I answered back, he called out a cheerful greeting and told me to tie up my horse and come in.

The main room of the cabin was lit by a single candle that sat on the table, so the back corners lay in darkness. As my eyes adjusted and I looked around, I saw Fernando sitting on the edge of a bunk, pulling on his boots. He got up and took a seat at the table, where Quico and I also sat down.

"Well, Yimi," said Quico, "what's new? Are you just out taking a look around?"

"Not really. I had a little trouble, and I thought I would come out and talk to you two about it."

"Oh, that's fine." He gave a brisk nod.

Fernando gave a slower nod but showed that he was paying attention.

I was thinking of how I was going to word things, when Quico spoke again.

"Would you like something to eat?"

I had smelled food when I first walked in. The smell of fried corn tortillas and melted pork fat hung on the air, and now with a little distance from my trouble, I could feel my appetite coming back. "Oh, I could eat a little, if it's not too much trouble."

"Not at all." Quico got up and set a greasy skillet on the stove. "Tell us about the problem," he said as he reached into the wood box for a couple of stove lengths.

"Well, you know, a little while back, a partner of mine got killed."

He turned his head and nodded at me. "Over there at the river."

"Yes. And then lately they came to try to get me. But they didn't have any luck. Actually, they had bad luck."

"Oh? More than one?"

"Uh-huh. One man and then another."

Quico raised his eyebrows. "Where did they come from?"

"It's strange. They were men I worked with."

"Oh, really? What reason would they have?"

"That's the thing I don't understand. The big boss, Whitlow, must have told them to do it, but I don't understand the whole reason."

Quico looked at Fernando and then at me. "Do you think it has something to do with that girl?"

"I don't know. It seems there's some other boss there, at the lodging house. But if there's a connection between him and my boss, I still don't see it."

Quico shrugged. "What's his name?"

"His last name is Melva." I looked at both of them, and they shook their heads. "I need to find out anything I can about either one of these two bosses." I watched as Quico spooned bacon grease from a can into the skillet. Then I said, "By the way, did you know that the girl went back to the other place?"

Quico set down the grease can, and Fernando sat up in his chair. "Where did she go to?" Quico asked.

"To the place where she was staying. This Melva is the owner of the guest house. I think she was afraid, so she went back there. But it doesn't make enough sense, and if I knew more about him, I might understand things better."

Quico tossed a tortilla into the grease, and it sputtered. "We can be on the lookout. There's gossip here and there. We can ask." He looked at Fernando, who nodded.

"I appreciate it."

"That's fine."

"And if you hear anything about that boss of mine, Whitlow, I'd like to know that, too."

"Sure."

Fernando spoke up. "Are you going back to the ranch tonight?"

"No. I don't think I'll go back at all."

Quico poked at the tortilla with a fork. "Do you want to stay here?"

I gave a half-smile. "I was hoping so. If it's not too much trouble."

"I don't think so. How many are there?"

"Of the sons of bitches?"

"Yes."

"Well, there are two of them that aren't going to do anything more. I don't know how many others there are."

Quico smiled. "There are three of us. Let the sons of bitches come." He nodded to Fernando. "Can you show him the corral for his horse while I heat the food?" Then he looked at me. "Did you talk to my uncle?"

"Some. He told me about the girl, that she had gone back. But the other part, about the two that tried to give me the business, some of that happened after I saw him." I left Nena out of it, not because these fellows would think she was the delicate kind of woman who didn't need to know about this kind of thing, but because she and I had already agreed it would be simpler if I didn't have to tell anyone that I had given Rudd his surprise in Nena's backyard. As long as Whitlow was still a threat, no one needed to know she was a witness.

Quico nodded. "I think it's good for my uncle to know what's going on. That way he can be on the lookout, too."

"Oh, yes. If you see him before I do, it won't bother me if you tell him what you know."

Fernando stood up and led the way outside, where I untied my horse and led him to the corral. Fernando gave the horse some oats and then helped me carry my gear back to the cabin. As I stepped inside, I caught the smell of tortillas and beans, and I was happy to be in the sheep camp.

Not too long after I had finished eating, I rolled my bedding out onto the floor. I took off my boots, my gunbelt, and my knife and set them aside. Then I put my pocket change in my hat and set it by the side of my bed as well. Some fellows put their things in their boots at night, but I never did, not even when I felt safe like I did at the moment. I liked to be able to get my boots on in an instant if I needed to.

Before long I could hear the even breathing of my two *compañeros*. It had been a long day for me, and I was tired, but I had too much going through my mind to go to sleep right away. Two men had tried to kill me, and the more I thought about it, the more it seemed connected to Helen. Whatever it was, it ran deeper than I could see.

As I lay in my bed on the floor, I got to thinking again about how Helen must have fallen into this fellow's hands. Like a peach. I remembered a tramp telling me one time, when we had climbed a fence to get into someone's garden, that it always tasted better when it was stolen. I had thought that was a cute saying and had used it a few times since then. I think it was probably true when a fellow enjoyed stealing things. Now I tried the idea out on the adventure I had had with Helen. It didn't seem as if I was getting a thrill from stealing someone else's peaches. It seemed as if it was just the two of us, her and me, and no one else in the picture. It had been a powerful sensation to feel her giving herself to me, but it did seem to be just between the two of us. The other fellow wouldn't see it that way, of course. He would think it was still his, and that idea would run so strong in him that he would strike hard if things seemed to be getting out of his hands. There I was, back to his hands again. I wished to hell I could see his face.

In the morning we had fried potatoes from one skillet and *chorizo* from another, with a pot of strong coffee to wash it all down. The *chorizo* was a spicy sausage, reddish orange inside, the likes of which I had seen hanging in Chanate's butcher shop. As far as I knew, it was usually made of pork, so I imagined it came from town and not from there at the sheep camp. All in all it was a good tasty meal, hot in both senses of the word, and likely to kill any bugs that were trying to set up business in a fellow's stomach or liver.

After breakfast, Quico and Fernando went about their day's work. They ran the camp, which was a sort of outpost for a big outfit farther south. They were in charge of hauling supplies out to the sheepherders, taking meat animals into town, and taking care of any sheep or larger livestock, such as horses and mules, that they had in the pens. I never envied a sheepherder's job, spending long months at a time with only a dog and an army of range maggots for company, but running a sheep camp didn't seem so bad. These lads had fresh food once in a while, had a place to get out of the weather, and got to go into town once in a while. I wouldn't care to have the oily smell of sheep in my nostrils all the time, but I saw it as honest work that let a fellow sleep at night.

Then I recalled how Rudd and Turner,

who were plenty crooked, had slept pretty well themselves when we were all at the boar's nest. So I concluded it wasn't just the work that made the difference, but how a fellow felt about it. Working with sheep wouldn't guarantee that a fellow would go straight, and now that I thought of it, some people had been known to steal sheep. I could go back to working at a cattle ranch, as long as it was on the up-and-up. It wasn't the cattle that led me astray; it was my own weakness. The good thing was that I could see what was wrong now and that I was making my break away from the crooked life.

As Quico and Fernando went about their work, I decided to go out on a ride. I hadn't yet decided for sure that I wasn't going to make a run for it. I felt the tug of that girl back in town, but I could also hear a little voice telling me not to stake too much on her. I thought I had a day or two to sort things out. It would take Whitlow a while to learn how things had gone wrong, and then it would take him a while longer to try to find out where I was and to decide how to go after me. By then I should have made my move.

I was used to riding out and snooping around anyway, and since I was just a few miles from the Kite, I thought I might drift over that way, quiet-like, to see what I could see. It occurred to me that I was spying on the fellow I used to spy for, and just like always, I had to be looking over my shoulder. I didn't know the men who worked for Whitlow at his other places, so I didn't know who to be on the lookout for. I didn't think anyone would be out hunting for me yet, and I didn't imagine they would expect me to be over this way. But all the same, I figured I had to be wary of anyone except Quico, Fernando, or one of their Mexican sheepherders.

I rode through a country of rolling foothills, dotted here and there with pine and juniper. It was good grass country — a bit rocky in places — and quite a bit of it was open range that both the cattlemen and the sheepmen thought belonged to them. I knew that the sheep usually stayed together, while the cattle wandered off in little bunches. I didn't see any sheep on my ride, but I did see cattle now and then.

It was the kind of country where I could get up on the crest of a hill and see for miles, especially off to the east, where the land sloped away to the plains. But even from a hilltop, I didn't know who or what might be lurking within half a mile. And when I was on a high point, I felt that all I was doing was making myself more visible. Most of the time, then, I looked for vantage points where the horse and I could blend in with a small stand of trees or a clump of rocks.

At one point I found a good lookout on a high spot, and I got off the horse and sat for a while. I had a fair idea of where I was, in relation to other places. The Kite would be off to the southwest. In back of me, almost due east from Whitlow's headquarters, would be the line camp where I had stayed until lately. Off to the north, and a little bit east, lay the town of Monetta. As for people, I imagined Turner's body had been hauled back to the boar's nest, unless Rudd buried him where he found him. Rudd was probably still lying on his back at Red Wind Crossing. Helen would be within the four walls of Maudenwarlick's nunnery, and Magdalena would be on this side of the river, free to come and go as she pleased, and probably trying not to think about the bloodstain in her backyard. The one person I had to worry about, or at least could put a face on, could be anywhere. I imagined that sometime today, he would go looking for Rudd.

Whatever Whitlow's original reasons

were for wanting to have me put out of the way, he had two more now — or he would by the time he came after me. If I knew where he was, I could stay one jump ahead of him and clear out of this place in time. As I pictured it, there was a big triangle between his place, the line camp, and the crossing. I expected he would be riding that triangle somewhere. He might even go into town, though I had gathered that he didn't go there much. I figured the sheep camp was as safe a place as any for me to hole up, but if I stayed hidden I wasn't going to learn anything, and even when I thought I was in a safe place, I could get a surprise — like the way Rudd had showed up.

Sitting there on that hillside felt somewhat like looking for deer. A fellow could do it in different ways — stay in one place and hope the deer came by, keep on the move and hope to cross paths with the deer, or combine the two, as I was doing. The one thing a fellow shouldn't do was go hide from what he was trying to find. My problem was that even if I found what I was looking for, I wouldn't know until then what I was going to do. What I was doing now was a lot more complicated than sitting by the outhouse and waiting for Iris the *enanita*. That had been as simple as waiting for a doe to step out of the cornfield and walk down to the spring, though not as graceful to watch.

I yawned as I watched the landscape around me. I tried to imagine Whitlow with a set of antlers on his head, but that didn't help much. I wasn't looking to shoot him, I didn't think. I just wanted to know where he was. That realization in itself gave me a warning. If Whitlow saw me first, he wouldn't think twice about putting a bullet through me. I told myself I had better not make the same mistake Turner did. If it came right down to it, I would have to have my mind set on staying alive.

As I sat there, my thoughts drifted again, from one thing to another. Of course, I got to thinking about that girl some more. From the couple of times I had been with her, I felt pulled into a powerful current. When I felt I was in control, it was a strong feeling. I imagined that the other fellow knew that feeling even better. After all, he was the kingpin. That was what Tome had called him. It seemed like a funny word as I sat there, running things through my head. A kingpin reminded me of a king stud, like they use in building houses. I remembered seeing a book of drawings of different kinds of structures, like houses and ships, and the words had a sort of magic to them. There were the king studs, which were uprights, and then on the roof trusses there were the queen posts. In another part of the book I saw a king post, which was a thick timber that supported several others that went out in different directions, like spokes from a hub. This kingpin fellow must be some kind of a king stud, I thought, or maybe even a king post, and poor Helen was just a little queen post, nailed into place.

I sat at my lookout, or stand, for about half an hour, thinking off and on about cute things like that, but always making myself come back to the serious matter at hand. The sun had climbed about halfway up in the sky, and I was starting to get drowsy. I thought I should get up and move around a little before I found another spot to settle into. Just as I was starting to stir, my horse made a snuffle sound. His ears went up, and I followed his gaze to the north to see what had alerted him.

It was a horse and rider, coming from the general direction of the town and headed, it seemed, in the direction of Whitlow's place. The object was at least a mile off, but I could see that the rider's upper body was dark, like Whitlow's frock coat.

I felt my heartbeat pick up, so I took a couple of deep breaths and made myself calm down. First I needed to see who it was, and then I could decide what to do. The rider was passing through a wide area between two hills, but I could see that he would be closed off from my view in another minute or so. I was going to have to move closer to get another peek.

From where I sat, it looked as if two or maybe three hills lay between my lookout and the trail the fellow was riding. I thought it would be best to go on foot, so that I wouldn't have the risk of my horse whinnying at the other. If it was Whitlow, he might even be riding one of the horses I had delivered, in which case the two horses would know each other and be more likely to make a noise. I could lead my horse partway, but then I didn't know if I would find a place to tie him up. And I had a good spot where he was.

The rider disappeared from my view. I had to get going if I was going to get another look. Then I wondered if I should carry my rifle. I would have some explaining to do if someone rode up on me while I was creeping along with every appearance of stalking another man. On the other hand, I would be a complete fool not to have it if things did come to a show-down. *To hell with appearances,* I thought. *These sons of bitches killed Jimmy Rooks, and they tried to kill me.* I pulled the rifle from the scabbard and started side-hilling my way down from my perch.

I went down the slope and up the other side in good time, slowing only as I came to the top, to make sure no one was looking my way. I saw nothing. Then I went down and up the next hill, again cresting it in slow steps. I figured the rider would be beyond the next rise and maybe a little ahead on the trail, so I headed downhill to my left and kept going in the same direction as I climbed the slope.

When I got near the top, I took off my hat and hunkered down. Leaving my hat behind me, I crawled forward until my field of vision cleared the top of the ridge.

My heart jumped as I saw the rider below me, riding off to my left at a fast walk. It was Whitlow, all right, in his frock coat. The back of it gave me a dark, broad object as I settled into a shooting position and lined up the sights. I did not lever in a shell because I had not yet decided whether I was going to shoot, but I knew I would do either one thing or the other when I got the feeling of having my sights lined up between his shoulder blades.

I could have done it. He was a hundred and fifty yards away, at the most, and I held the sights steady on him for ten or fifteen seconds, then relaxed, and then held steady again. I could have put him out of the way, settled this whole thing with Jimmy Rooks, and left myself clear to go back to town and hash things out with Helen and her keepers. But I didn't. Even if no one else ever knew, I felt it would be shameful to shoot Whitlow in the back. If I could get him face-on, especially if he came at me first, that would be different. But not this way. I didn't want to do it badly enough, and when that was the case, a fellow didn't always make a good shot, even when he knew he was holding steady. I was sure I could knock him out of the saddle, but a little voice told me not to try, so it was just as well that I didn't.

As I scuttled back down the hill, I realized I had gotten something done anyway. I knew where the boss man was headed, and I could go in the opposite direction. I could go back to the sheep camp, check in with the boys, fetch my gear, and head for Red Wind Crossing.

Chapter Thirteen

I made it to the crossing in the early afternoon, and Rudd's body was gone. From that, I imagined Whitlow must have been waiting to hear from Rudd, and when he didn't, he either went out looking or sent someone else to do it. Because he seemed to be coming from town when I saw him, I doubted that he would have hauled Rudd out to the line camp and then taken the long way home. I doubted even more that he would have brought Rudd into town. So, I figured, either he had someone else picking up the pieces, which he could well have done if he had gotten a warning from Rudd after Turner failed, or someone else was in on this whole mess. That was a possibility I hadn't considered except in the dimmest way. Rudd and Turner could have been working for two different bosses.

My head was starting to spin, so I made myself think things through in a straight line. Rudd had said Jimmy Rooks crossed the boss, but he didn't say which one. That was true. But it coincided with Whitlow's warning that a man didn't cross this outfit.

And then it wasn't until Whitlow showed up with a change of plans, and talked to Rudd and Turner in the boar's nest when I was outside, that the other two started coming after me. So all of this came through Whitlow, even if there was a bigger boss above him. If there was, I still had Whitlow to look out for, and if there was anyone else tending to this business, such as going around picking up bodies, it didn't matter very much whether he was working for Whitlow or Darcy Melva. I had to be on the lookout for him, too.

Warlick, for instance — I could imagine someone telling him to take Rudd to the line camp. From what Helen had said, he had hauled dead bodies before, and from the picture I had of him, he seemed like a good one to act as an amateur undertaker.

But it could be just about anybody, except for Tome, Goings, and my Mexican friends. The main idea I was forming was that I had more than Whitlow to deal with and that I had better settle my affairs one way or the other and get out while I could.

By now I knew that the main reason I hadn't made a run for it was that I had to find out about the girl. I needed to know if she was willing to go with me, and as Tome and Nena's comments gnawed on me, I knew I also had to decide whether she was worth the trouble. And I couldn't do that until I knew how this fellow Darcy Melva had such a hold on her and kept her shoes nailed to the floor. Again, I tried to think these things out in a straight line, but they tried to go around in a circle on me, so I just decided I needed to find out about the girl. Whatever that meant, as far as what I was going to learn and in what order, I could do it and then move on.

The more I thought about Helen, the more it seemed she was kept under some kind of a strange power. I remembered reading a story once, at some time back when I was in school and liked to learn things and be smart in front of the girls. The story was about a maiden who was being kept prisoner in a castle. The master didn't have her under lock and key because he didn't want anyone to be able to say he was keeping her against her will. Instead, he held her with some kind of a potion that kept her under a spell, so she wasn't able to walk away. She could walk around inside the castle, but if she tried to go out into the forest, the spell brought her back. Sure enough, in the story a knight came along and saw that she needed rescuing. He made his way into the castle, chased around inside the passageways and such, and finally carried her out in his arms. He took the potion to a sorcerer or an alchemist or something, and he found out it was a poison that kept her groggy in small doses but that would eventually kill her if it didn't get cleaned out of her blood. I remember the story well, although I couldn't have been more than twelve when I read it.

Now, as I rode into Monetta, reminding myself again to keep my wits about me and not slip too far into my daydreams, I thought that Helen was like the girl in the story. I could be like the knight who rescued her. Then I reminded myself that all I was was Jimmy Clevis, not much better than the saddle tramp that Maud said I was, but hoping to get out of this life of being a sneak and a thief. And if I was going to live long enough to do that, I had better pull my head out of the clouds — or wherever it had been. I couldn't kid myself on that score. I knew I had been drawn in by the power of what she and I had done in the dark, and I needed to keep that from being a potion that kept me in a daze. If I didn't, I could end up just one more saddle tramp with a bullet put through him, without even knowing whose direction it came from. But I also knew I wanted more of what I had sampled, and that was part of the reason I was going to Monetta.

When I saw the town up ahead, I realized I was riding straight for the boardinghouse without having given any thought to going through Mexican town first. I wished I had thought of it sooner. I could have dropped in to see how Magdalena was doing, and I could have let Chanate know more about my troubles with Whitlow's men. I told myself I could go there after I found out more about the girl.

Once I got into town, I decided to ride past the back of the boardinghouse first. As I rode down the alleyway and reined in by the corn crib, I saw that I might be in luck. Iris the *enanita* was in the middle of the backyard, doing battle with a rug that was draped over the clothesline. It was a big rug, about six feet wide and hanging about four feet down on each side. I wondered if she had hung up the rug by herself or if sturdy Warlick had helped her. It outsized her pretty well. She was giving it furious licks with a rug beater, that kind of flail made of welded iron rods. With each swing, she would lean into the stroke with both hands and then stop dead as the flail raised a puff of dust from the rug. Then she would rock back on her heels, raise her weapon, and give the rug another blow.

I got down from my horse and walked to the side of the shed. When she finished her next swing, I whistled. When she looked my way, she lowered the rug beater and heaved out a long breath. I beckoned to her, and she came walking over, a little more off-balance than usual, it seemed, because of the tool she was carrying.

"Hello there, Iris. It looks like they've got you working, like always."

"They sure do." She stopped in front of me, rested the heavy end of the rug beater on the ground, and looked up with her washed-out blue eyes.

"How did you get that rug up onto the clothesline?"

"Maud helped me." She showed her short teeth as she took an openmouthed breath. She reminded me, just for a second, of a dog panting.

"It looks like hard work."

"It is."

"But you're used to hard work, aren't you?"

"I sure am. They make me do everything. Sweep and mop, clean the rooms, serve the meals, and do the dishes. Then, in between times, they have me do things like this."

"Uh-huh. No help, then?"

"Nope."

She moved the beater to her left hand and lowered her head as if to give it a rest. I saw the part in her hair running down the middle of her scalp, with the rows of tight curls running on either side. Everything about her seemed normal to me now, and I don't believe a shackle around her neck would have surprised me.

"Well, that's too bad. A working girl like you deserves to be treated better."

She looked up and showed her teeth again. "You want to see Helen, don't you?"

"Um, yeah. Of course I do."

"I thought so. Whenever you start saying nice things to me, that's what you want."

"Maybe so. But that doesn't mean I don't care about you, Iris, or that I don't wish they would get someone to help you."

She closed her mouth and pushed her lower lip against her upper.

I winked at her. "You know, I think you're just in a pout because you haven't been able to get out of here long enough to have an ice cream. Am I right about that part?"

She waited a moment before she answered. "Maybe."

"Well, I wouldn't worry about it if I were

you. Things'll change, sooner or later, and if you just sack up your quarters in the meanwhile, you'll be all set when the time comes. Don't you think?"

"Maybe."

"So I'll tell you what. I'll give you two of these today." I held out two quarters between my thumb and my first two fingers. "One from me, and one from the other fellow. He couldn't make it anymore."

"You mean the man with the tall boots?"

I cleared my throat. "Um, no, not him. I mean the other boy, the one about my age. The one with brown eyes, name of Jimmy."

She shook her head. "Never saw him. Never heard of him."

"Well, take 'em both anyway. He would want you to. He was a friend of mine, but he went away." As I waited for her to do something, I had another thought. "How about the man with the tall boots? Did he ask about me?"

"I don't know. He didn't talk to me."

"Oh, did he talk to Helen?"

"No. To Warlick."

"Ah-hah. Well, then, of course he wouldn't have anything for you. He was too tightfisted. But the other boy was nice."

She shrugged. "I don't know. I never met him."

"Take my word for it. He would want you to have both of these." I moved the coins closer toward her.

She took them and closed her small hand around them. "Helen said to tell you, if you came back, that she can see you after dark. In the same place as before."

"Not by the back door."

"No. Out here." She lifted her square little chin and motioned toward the shed.

"Thanks, Iris. You're a good girl. Tell Helen I'll be here right at dark and I'll wait for her."

"All right."

She returned to her work, and I went back to my horse. As I rode away, I could hear the soft thuds of the *enanita* waging war on the rug.

With a little time on my hands, I thought I might go to the Jack-Deuce and see if Goings had raised anything. Then I decided I didn't like the idea of leaving the horse out on the main street as an advertisement of my whereabouts, so I went to the smaller of the two stables in town and left the horse there. The stableman looked over the horse and the brand but said nothing more than the usual. I paid him ahead of time, thinking I might want to leave on short order, and then I went on my way on foot.

Inside the Jack-Deuce, I found Tome and Goings at the same table as usual, looking as if they had never left. I ordered a glass of beer and carried it over to sit with them.

Tome's voice was as crisp as always. "How goes it, Galahad?"

"Oh, just fine. Any news?"

Tome shook his head. "Haven't heard anything."

I looked at Goings. "How about you? Did you get to see anything?"

"He didn't get to see the little kitten," said Tome.

"No, but I got to see the inside of the place like you wanted."

"Oh, good. Was it hard to get in?"

"Not really. I just wandered in, like you said. The old whore caught me and asked what I was doing there, and then she said they had plenty of help, and she showed me to the door."

"When was that?"

"Just a couple of hours ago. There was someone in the front part when I went by yesterday, so I decided to try again when there was no one out there."

"Good idea."

"Uh-huh. It worked all right."

"Did you catch a look at whoever was in there the first time you went by?"

"No, not really."

"Oh, well. That doesn't matter." It would have been good to know, but I had to toss it away and get back to the main point. "So, what does the place look like?"

"Well, that first room is just a little sitting room, with a desk and a few seats. You go through it and come to a door, which opens onto a hallway going crosswise. Off to the right is the dining room, and back around from there, in the corner of the building near the street, is the kitchen. Back down the hallway to the left, you turn right and go into a parlor. That's where they have couches, a piano, a chandelier, and all. That's the part that looks like a whorehouse. It's a good-sized room."

"What's in the corner by the street, then — the left-hand corner as you look at the building from the front?"

"I don't know. Probably a water closet. It's not in the right place for a cloakroom, but it could be that, too."

"Does the parlor reach all the way to the back door? I wouldn't think so."

"No, it doesn't."

"So wouldn't the water closet be closer to the back door?"

"Probably so, now that you mention it. And that room in front could be a cloak-room or some little storage room."

"How far back does the parlor go?"

"Over halfway. At the far end of it, there's a stairway that leads upstairs."

"So there are probably sleeping rooms on the ground floor as well as upstairs."

"I imagine so."

Tome spoke up. "The old bitch and the whoremaster probably live on the ground floor, with the girls upstairs."

I nodded and looked back at Goings. "So there's a door at the far end of the parlor, leading to the back part of the building, where you might find the water closet and the back door?"

"Right. I would imagine there's a little hallway there."

"And the foot of the stairway is some-where near that door?"

Goings looked at his eyebrows for a second. "That's right. You know, I saw as much as I could in a short while, and I think that's pretty accurate."

"Good enough. I may not need to know any of it, but if I do, even a general idea will help. I appreciate it. I hope it wasn't much trouble."

"Not much at all. The hardest part was

lookin' at the old whore up close."

Tome laughed. "She's a fright, isn't she?" Then he looked at me. "If you don't get your little puss out of there, she'll look like that some day. That's assuming you can get her out."

"Nice of you to mention it," I said. "But I don't even know if she wants to leave. For all I know, that other fellow's got a deep hold on her."

"That doesn't sound good, either," said Tome.

"I know. But I've got to find out."

Evening found me sitting in the murky dusk. Now that I had some idea of the interior of the place, I spent a little time imagining what I might find if I went in the back door. There would probably be a hallway, with a water closet on one side and maybe a bath on the other, or the two of them side by side. The hallway would lead into the parlor, and once inside there, I would find the stairway. If I didn't go that far, I would probably find more rooms off to my left, maybe with another hallway leading to them. I thought Tome's guess as to who lived upstairs and who lived down was a pretty good one. As for the little kitten, as he called Iris, I imagined she had a room in the back, near the bath and the laundry room and all of that. If Helen came down the stairway and out the back door, she would go past those rooms. She might even use one of the rooms as an excuse to come downstairs.

When I tried to picture the upstairs, I had no idea. A building that big, with lodging rooms on the second floor, was likely to have two hallways running its length, with at least one hall running crossways. But for all I knew, it could be cut up and laid out in any of several other ways. If I had to go up there, I would just find out then what kind of a maze it was.

I hadn't sat very long when the back door of the building opened and out stepped Helen. I could see her blond hair and light-colored dress in the moonlight, and my pulse quickened as I stood up to meet her.

She fell into my arms right away, and we met in a long kiss. When we finally separated, she spoke.

"I'm so glad you came back. I was afraid I might not see you again."

I kissed her hair. "It wasn't easy. I've had other troubles, but I had to come back and see you."

She pressed the side of her face against

my chest. "I'm glad you did. I had to see you again."

I raised my hand to her head and stroked her hair. "I want to get you away from here, Helen. We can go someplace else, just the two of us. We can get away from everything that has plagued us both."

"I'd like that."

My heart gave a little skip. "Do you think you could? Right now?"

"I don't know about right now. I think I have to wait just a little while."

"You mean until later this evening?"

"Um, no. I guess I mean after this evening. I need to wait a little."

"What for? To get your nerve up?"

"No." She let out a quick, short breath. "I need a little more time to — recover, I guess."

"You mean from trying to run away and not making it?"

"Well, that."

"Something else, then? Is it him?"

"Yes, it's him."

"Did he do something to you?"

"Um, no."

"Well, what is it, then?"

She buried her head against my chest. "I don't know. It's just that when he comes by, I'm not any good for a while."

"You mean he just takes it all out of you?"

"Yeah, I guess so. It takes me a few days to build up again."

I remembered how I had gotten her to leave before, and I wondered if it would work again. From the sounds of it, he had been back in the meanwhile. I thought that if I could cover her, I might be able to rub out his effect a little quicker. I lowered my hand to her hip, and she didn't resist.

"Would you like to be mine again, Helen?"

"Yes, but not right now."

"Later? When we go away?"

"Maybe later."

"Later tonight?"

"I don't know."

I was burning up where I pressed against her. I could feel it, and I was sure she could feel it, too. "What is it?" I asked.

"I don't know. I'm just not any good."

"It's him, isn't it? You want me, but he won't let you, and he's not even here. Is that it?"

"I think so."

"My God, Helen. I've got to get you out of here. Why don't you just go away with me right now?"

"I want to, but I can't."

"You can if you want. All you have to do is want to."

She shook her head, and I could feel her sobbing.

"What is it, darling? Tell me. Please."

"I'm no good. I'm just no good."

"Of course you are."

"No, I'm not."

"It's not you," I said. "It's what he's done to you."

She had quit sobbing, but she didn't say anything.

"I can tell," I went on. "He's got you scared to death. He's got you convinced that he owns you, hasn't he?"

"Not really."

"Well, I think it's something like that, or you could just get up and leave."

"It's not that easy."

I thought for a few seconds. "Let me put it this way. He thinks you're his, doesn't he?"

"I guess so."

"He made you his, the way I did, but he wasn't nice about it. And that's why you're afraid."

She sobbed again, and I could feel her tears through my shirt. I knew I was right about how he had her. I wanted more than anything to break his spell, but I could tell I was pushing up against a wall. When she didn't say anything, I spoke again.

"You're afraid because of the way he did it, or the way he has done it since then. Am I right?"

Finally she spoke. "He took me when I was still pretty young. As he liked to put it, he broke me in. And after what he's done, I don't think I would be any good to you."

I shrugged. "I can live with any of that. And as far as that goes, you would be plenty good."

She shook her head. "No, he's in me, and I can't get him out."

I felt a chill. "Do you mean you're carrying his baby?"

"No."

She didn't sound very definite, so I said, "Are you sure?"

"Yes, I'm sure. Now."

I squinted, trying to find the answer in the dark. "Does that mean you might have, at one time?"

She didn't speak for a long moment, but I thought she wanted to, so I waited. She took a few long shuddering breaths, and then she spoke.

"I'm not carrying his baby now, but I did at one time, and he took it away from me."

"You mean he gave it to someone else?"

"No. He just took it."

"Right after it was born?"

She started crying, and I stroked her hair until she calmed down.

"It's all right," I said. "You don't have to tell me any more than you want to."

"I might as well. There's not much more, but it's the worst."

"Well, go ahead."

"He beat me on the stomach and made me lose it."

I could feel the blood drain from my face. "Why would he do that?"

"I told him I didn't know if I wanted to have his baby, and he went into a rage. And then he left me alone until it was all over. He didn't help me with any of it."

"My God," I said. "You could have him put away for that."

She shook her head. "He's told me it would just be his word against mine. And I know that if I tried anything, he would just make it worse on me."

"Uh-huh. And how long ago was this?"

"It was early on. At the beginning."

"When you were young. How old were you?"

"Seventeen."

"I see. And he's had control of your life ever since."

"Just about."

"By that you mean the part about being with me?"

"Well, that too, but what I meant was that I went back to live with my mother for a while. My father had already passed on. Then, when she did, I didn't have anyplace else to go, or I didn't think I did."

"But even when you went back to live with your mother, you weren't leaving him. He left you to suffer through what he did to you, but he still had a hold on you, or you wouldn't have gone back to him. You couldn't leave him."

"I didn't think I could. So, no, I guess I couldn't."

"How old were you when you went back, then?"

"After my mother passed away? Just eighteen."

I gave a low whistle. "And I suppose he's let you know what he would do if you tried to leave. Or have you?"

"Once. When he got me back, he let me know then."

"You mean he took you by force?"

She didn't answer.

"He did, didn't he?"

She still said nothing.

"I know he did. You as much as said so. Did he beat you, too?"

"He didn't have to. He knew how to humiliate me. After he did what he wanted in private, he cut off all my hair, short, so I couldn't go out and about."

"Like a jail dock?"

"What's that?"

"It's what they give prisoners. They shear it off close, all the way around, like a sheep."

"That's what he did."

"And you haven't tried since, except with me?"

"I've wanted to. But all he has to do is come around, and I'm no good."

I was quiet for a long moment as I searched for words. "Does he make you feel ashamed?"

"Yes."

"But I would guess he's not ashamed of any of it."

"He doesn't seem to be."

"Yet you are. He dumps it all on you, and you accept it."

"I can't help it."

"Well, let me ask you this. Were you ashamed of what you did with me?"

She looked at me, serious and clear as could be. "Not at all."

I kissed her. "See? It's all clean and natural, if you do it right." I motioned with

270

my hand. "You and me."

She buried her head on my chest again. "I wish I could. But I feel that it's lost."

"That what is?"

"That all of it is lost. My innocence, and whatever was clean and natural. It's all been twisted and forced and coerced."

"And it doesn't bother him."

"It doesn't seem to."

"Does he seem to enjoy watching you suffer?"

"It seems like it. At least to the extent that it keeps me under his thumb."

"Then why in the hell don't you just get out?"

"I don't know. I can't."

"But you want out."

"I wish I could."

"Does he know you tried to leave the other night?"

"He knows I went away for a little while, but he doesn't know where."

"Does he know about me?"

"Not from me. I haven't given him your name. But he might have gotten it from Maud."

"Hmm. Did I say it in front of her that day?"

"Yes, you did."

"Well, it's too late to do anything about

that. But he doesn't know you went off with me?"

"I didn't tell him. But he does know I was gone for a while, and he didn't like it."

"Did he do something? Did he beat you?"

"He didn't beat me."

"Oh." I could imagine the rest, or at least I thought I could. She had already hinted at it once. Whatever he had done, she hadn't gotten over it. "But he's not here now?"

"No."

"And you still can't leave?"

She shook her head. "I just . . . I don't know. I can't. Not right now."

"But you want to?"

"Yes."

"You want out for good."

"Yes."

"And you want me to help you?"

"Yes."

I had my hand on her buttock again. My strength had faded away, but I could feel it surging back again. "When can you be mine again?"

"Soon."

I realized I was doing most of the talking at this point, and she was just agreeing, but it gave me encouragement. I lifted her face to mine in the moonlight. Her eyes were wet and shiny, and I thought I could see hope in her face.

We met in a long, moist kiss as I held her tight at the waist with my left hand and rubbed her rump with my right. Then we came apart at the sound of the back door opening.

The lowered voice of the *enanita* traveled across the yard in the evening air. "Helen. You'd better come in."

Chapter Fourteen

I didn't like being left standing by the out-house like that, feeling like a sneak, just because the girl was afraid. This Darcy Melva fellow sounded like strong poison, but from what I had heard, he was mainly a black-mailer and a rapist, with a little bit of the woman-beater as well. That made him something for her to be afraid of, but from my point of view, it also shaped him up as a kind of coward. I wasn't going to be afraid of someone I hadn't even seen yet. It was like what they said about being afraid of your own shadow — or someone else's, as in this instance.

It put me in mind of a story the teacher had read to us in the second or third grade. There was a family — a man, a woman, and their daughter — and they had a little inn or tavern. At one point the girl was supposed to go down into the cellar to draw some beer, and she saw a mallet hanging above the doorway. She got all scared and came back to tell her mother, who said, "Give me the pitcher," and she went down and got a fright, too. Then the father tried, and he couldn't do anything either. Finally a stranger in the inn went down the stairs, took hold of the mallet, and got it out of the way. Then everybody could act normal again and draw beer and go on about their business. That story stuck with me for a long time. It impressed me with the fear these people had, how senseless it was and how it still paralyzed them.

That was how I saw Helen — just limp as a rag because of the threat that hung over her. Granted, the fellow had done some pretty cruel things, from the sound of it, but to me, at least, he was still something that could be dealt with. And I could be like the fellow in the story, who came in off the street and had the power to act. I can't remember if he got to marry the innkeeper's daughter, but if she was pretty, he should have.

So I stood out there in the dark for a while, until I said to hell with it. I was going to go up to the back door and see if I could hear anything. Just before I charged ahead, I had a clear moment and remembered I didn't have a horse nearby. It was several blocks away, and I didn't know if I might need to get away from that place in a hurry. So I walked to the stable, thinking that in the meanwhile I might just let things go. I could make my way back to Mexican town and decide whether to give it one more try or to give it up for good. But once I got the horse out of the stable, it seemed as if he went of his own accord right back to the alley behind the boardinghouse. I had taken off my spurs much earlier, so I moved nice and quiet as I tied him up to the corn crib, walked over to the shed, and stood there. I couldn't hear a thing from the house. I thought, *I'm going to settle this thing once and for all. She either does or doesn't.* So I walked across the yard, went up the steps with a soft tread, and stood by the back door. I tried it, and it was not locked.

My heart was thumping, partly out of nervousness and partly out of a feeling that something big might happen. If I could get in touch with her, and if she wanted, I could carry her right out of there. Then again, I knew I might just stand at the back door for an hour, on edge, and have nothing happen.

I stood there for a good fifteen minutes, hearing very little except for faint sounds of movement — footsteps, a closing door, a chair scraping on a wooden floor. Then I heard a series of sounds that seemed to be coming my way. It sounded as if someone might be coming from the parlor to the back area. I heard a woman's voice. I couldn't hear the words, but it sounded like a retort thrown back at someone, followed by a muffled sound from farther within. Then the steps came closer, and I heard the person say, "In a few minutes." It was Helen's voice.

I thought she might come outside, but she didn't. The footsteps came to a halt, and I heard a door open and close. I understood why she needed a few minutes, so I waited until I heard the door open. Now was the moment. I opened the back door and stepped inside. As I did it, I knew it was possible that I had been mistaken, that the voice I heard belonged to one of the other girls and I would have to get the hell out of there, fast. I had my hand ready at my six-gun. The door from the parlor stood ajar, and a dull light came through. As the person turned to see who had come in through the door, I saw from her profile that I had not made a mistake.

"Helen!" I whispered.

"What are you doing here?" Her voice was even quieter than mine.

"I came for you."

"You can't be in here."

"Well, I am."

"You've got to leave."

"No, I'm not going."

"Well, you can't —"

"I'm not leaving. Not yet. We're going to settle it here and now."

"Settle what?"

"Whether you're going to be mine and leave with me, or if you're going to stay here."

"I can't leave. Not now."

"Why? Is he here?"

"No, he's not. But I can't leave."

"Well, I didn't like the way I got left standing out there, and I want an answer."

"Please leave."

I had the feeling that I was on top for the moment, that I had the advantage. "Hell, no," I said. "If it's a matter of telling Maudenwarlick, I'll tell 'em." I walked past her in the dim hallway, and as I reached the door to the parlor, she whispered again.

"Please don't."

I stepped into the parlor, and it was empty. She was right behind me, and she took me by the arm and hurried me across the rug into the little room at the far end of the parlor. We stood in the dark for about a minute — stupid, it seemed to me — until I lit a match and found a candle in a brass holder. I lit it and then looked around. It was a storage room, with shelves and an old sideboard and a wooden chair. I looked at the door and saw a skeleton key sticking out of the lock.

"Why don't we lock the door?" I asked. "Just as a little safety measure."

As she turned the key, she said, "I can't stay here very long."

"Well, I doubt that I can stay here all night. Why did you bring us in here, anyway?"

"We had to get out of the way. I thought someone would hear us."

"Now that we're here, how do you think I'm going to get out of this place?"

"I don't know."

I laughed. "Helen, this is crazy." Then I saw the look on her face. "You're scared, aren't you?"

"Yes, I am."

"Why?"

"I'm afraid for you."

"What can happen to me?"

"The same thing that happened to your friend Jimmy."

"So this fella did have something to do with it."

"Jimmy, I'm *scared*."

I gave her a stern look. "Helen, this

cheap son of a bitch isn't going to harm a hair on your head. Not while I'm here."

Her hand went up to her head, and I remembered what she had told me about his cutting off all her hair.

"Look, honey," I said, "let's just get out of here."

"Jimmy, I *can't*."

"The hell you can't. What's he got?" I looked into her eyes, and she just stared back in fear. "Tell me," I said. "What's he got?"

Her eyes seemed to dull a little as she said, "He has part of me."

"Do you mean the baby?"

"No, he took that, but he doesn't have it."

"Well, then, what is it?"

"It's something he has. It's part of me that he carries around with him."

"What's that?"

"My hair."

I looked at her head. It was all there.

"No," she said. "The hair he cut off."

It all clicked and fell into place like the cylinder of a six-gun. Everything fit — the braid and the fob, the frock coat, the glare. Now I could see a face on Helen's master. The blackmailer and rapist was the same person as the thief who stole sheep and used someone else's brand. There weren't two people — just one, with different ways of walking all over others, getting inside their lives, rooting around, and taking what he wanted. Here I thought I was getting ready to deal with Darcy Melva, and I realized the two trails came together.

"The son of a bitch is here, isn't he?"

"Jimmy, if you would just leave. We can get you out the front door."

My blood felt colder now, but I wasn't going to run for it. Not at this point. I just needed to know what I was up against. "He's here, isn't he?"

At that moment, there was a rap on the panel of the door. Neither of us said anything, and the rap sounded again.

"Helen." It was the *enanita*'s voice. "Helen, he wants to see you in his room."

I looked at Helen, and she looked away.

"Helen, he wants to see you."

"Not just yet, Iris. I need a few minutes. Tell him I'll be there in a few minutes."

I heard the mutter of another voice, a male voice, and then the door handle rattled. I looked at the key in the lock and hoped it held fast. Then all of a sudden the door came crashing open as the doorjamb split. It was Warlick, bent over after putting all of his weight behind a charge with his left shoulder. Jumping back and taking the chair into my hands, I laid him out before he could get his head up.

I went to the doorway and looked out into the parlor, wondering where the master was. The *enanita* stood about ten feet back, with her fingers at her teeth.

"Where is he, Iris? Where's the man in the dark coat?"

"He's in the kitchen."

She wasn't a good liar. I could see her eyes roll back and to her left.

"I thought you said he wanted to see Helen in his room."

"Yes, I did, but he was in the kitchen when he told me."

"Having his cakes and ale, I suppose." I turned to Helen and reached out my hand. "Come on. I'm gettin' you out of here. If he wants to try to stop us, let him go ahead and try."

She looked down at Warlick, as if she was afraid of him as well.

"He's out now, but I think he'll come around," I said. "If Iris wants to, she can throw a bucket of water in his face." I reached out my left hand and helped Helen step over the *jorobado* who was slumped on the floor.

With my left hand leading her and my

right hand hovering over my pistol butt, I started to make the long walk across the parlor to the door at the foot of the staircase. Our steps were quiet on the rug, and no other sounds came from anywhere in the house. I had the feeling that whoever else was in the building was waiting — Maud and the girls were waiting for the master to do something, and he was waiting to get me.

I knew I had a clear run for the front door if I wanted it, but I was way past that. I had come this far, and there was only one way out for me — past the stairway.

I kept my eye on it as we stepped across the room. It was an open staircase on this side, with a newel post on the bottom and a handrail sloping upward behind the piano and disappearing at the ceiling.

When we were within four or five steps of the door, I thought I saw a faint shadow near the top of the stairs, but with a closer look I saw nothing.

Then I heard his voice, loud and terrible, ringing in the stairwell and the hall above. "Hel-len!"

She bolted and ran back toward Iris as the dark master came down the steps two at a time, his left hand on the banister and his right hand bringing a pistol up and around and pointed at me.

My gun was out and up, steady in my hand as I raised my arm and pulled the trigger. Gunfire split the air in the parlor — once, twice — and I couldn't tell which of us fired first. He reeled back, pulled himself up with his grip on the handrail, leaned forward, pointed his gun at me again, and pitched forward. He went over the banister, hit the piano with a thump and a thrum, and landed on the floor.

I looked around. Iris and Helen were standing by the cloakroom door. Maud, with a fireplace poker in her hand, stood by the door of the dining room, with two brown-haired girls in back of her. They looked like a dry doe and two young ones at the edge of a thicket. Turning back to the man who lay dead on the floor, I walked over and stood there. As I looked down at him, I saw Darcy Melva and Ed Whitlow both, come together in one form. It was the right man, in the right place.

He had landed facedown, with his head turned to the right. I couldn't see the watch chain, but as I looked in that area, I saw a stain of blood spreading out on the green rug. For all the trouble he had caused people, this was what he had come to — to die on the floor of his own whorehouse. I couldn't feel very sorry about that.

As I looked at him, I thought again of his two names. I could imagine why he took on a second identity. If things got too hot for him as Ed Whitlow, he could slip out of that identity and into another that he had waiting — like a banker might do when he came home in the evening, as he took off his business coat and put on his evening jacket.

I put my gun back in my holster and walked across the room to Helen. Iris sank back into the doorway of the storage room. "I don't think he'll be giving you any more trouble," I said to Helen.

She looked at me and gave me a slow, short nod.

"I think I have it figured out, but I'd like to make sure. Did you know this fellow by two different names?"

"Well, yes."

"He went by Whitlow when he got ahold of your father's brand, didn't he?"

"Yes, he did."

"Why did you call him by his summer name, then?"

"Because he told me to."

I raised my eyebrows. I felt like telling

her she could have saved us all a lot of trouble if she hadn't been protecting him, but I figured it was spilled milk. "Do you think you can leave now?" I asked.

"I think so. I don't see why not."

"Good. Let's get the hell out of here. We can come back for your things later."

After a glance at Maud and the other two girls, I took Helen by the hand and led her across the room and on out of the building. I would have expected her to show a little more emotion, or relief, at least, but she seemed to be in a daze. I led her through the backyard, between the outbuildings, and up to my horse. She stood by as I moved my bedroll and bag to the front of the saddle. When I got mounted up and had her in place behind me, I said, "Hang on." She did, without saying a word all the way to Red Wind Crossing.

We got there in good time and crossed the river in the moonlight. I got a campfire going and spread out the bedroll. She just sat on a rock and stared at the fire.

I was hoping she would give herself to me again, in a big trembling release, but she didn't yield to my touch. I asked her if she was sorry for what had happened to "him," and she said no. It was evident, though, that if she wasn't sorry, she sure wasn't happy, either. As nearly as I could tell, she was just numb. She had gone away with me, but her heart wasn't in it after all. She had tried, but she was just going through the motions.

I convinced her to lie down and cover up in the bedroll. I lay on the ground next to her, covered with a jacket, and I was able to go to sleep. I don't know if she slept. For all I knew, she may have spent the night lying on her back and staring up into the darkness.

Chapter Fifteen

In the morning she said she wanted to go back.

"You mean to that place?"

She shrugged. "It's the only place I know."

"Helen," I said, "you don't have to go back. You can stay with me. We can go somewhere."

She shook her head. "I don't feel like doing anything or going anywhere right now, so I think I might as well go back."

"You might want to think about it."

"I already have. I think it would be best."

"Because of what I did? To him?"

"No, because of me."

"What's wrong with *you?*"

"I don't know."

"I'd think it could be fixed."

"I don't know. I feel broken. I'm not ready to move on."

I shook my head as I took a deep breath and let it out. "My God, Helen, are you just going to sit down and quit?"

"For right now, I guess so. It's just the way I feel."

"Broken?"

"That's the only word I can think of right now."

"Well, I'm trying to understand that, but I can't see where feeling that there's something wrong with you should make you want to quit."

"I don't think you understand the feeling."

"Maybe not, but I understand something. I think there's a lot of us in this life who feel as if a piece or a chunk has been gouged out, or a hole has been put through us, but we try to patch it up, stitch it or pull it together, and let it scar over. I know it seems like there's a whole different class of people out there, people who are luckier or have more privilege, and they don't ever have to feel that way. They don't feel flawed like we do. But that's their luck. For the rest of us, we try to do the best we can with what we've got. Even if we've got a hole knocked in us, there's a lot in life we can enjoy."

"I wish I could feel that optimistic, but I don't have it in me."

"You mean right now? Until you can bounce back?"

She shook her head. "I don't have any bounce. I feel dead. I know I'm not, but I also know I can't go anywhere. It's as if I lost my legs, and I don't know how long it will be until I get them back."

"I wish I could help."

"I wish you could, too. But it doesn't work."

I kissed her, and she kissed me back, but I could tell there wasn't much in it. Well, I thought, at least I found out.

We got loaded up on the horse again, and I took her back to town. I left her off at the back door, and without paying my respects to any of the rest of the crew, I rode away. After everything that had happened, I left with an empty feeling, too. Even though she chose to go back there, I felt sorry for her. This fellow, call him by one name or another, had dragged her through quite a bit. He had taken something young and unspoiled and had corrupted it. He had gotten his hands on what was natural in her and had twisted it to suit his own self-centered purposes. He had given her quite a thrashing, and she would be a long time getting over it.

It seemed as if I was a ways ahead of her on the trail, as if she and I were at different stages in our journeys. When I knew I wanted to get out of my life of secrecy and shame, I was ready to follow through.

Whatever being a thief had held for me — feeling bold, thinking I was clever, or putting myself on an equal footing with people who had more — I was through with it. But she wasn't that far along. She knew she wanted out, but she wasn't ready to do what she had to do to stay free. The secrets he worked on her had more power than the ones that had held me, probably because they carried more shame, and she couldn't just slough it all off. It was inside her, like traces of poison. Some of it, like the tension and the urgency, she had transmitted to me, and from the little I had felt, I could imagine how the dread and the shame still ran in her blood. I had been on a ten-day drunk one time, and it took me a good week to work it all out of me. I had known men who had been drunk for months on end, or bleary for years, and I wondered how long it would take one of them to clean out his system and get back on his feet for real. That was how I saw Helen now — off to a shaky start, with most of the road ahead of her.

I felt I had done what I could. I had thought I was taking charge when I went into that house to settle things, but now I could see that I could go only so far. Even if I carried her like the prince did in the story, she was going to have to walk on her own two feet. She was going to have to get that sick son of a bitch out of her blood by herself, and there was no telling how long it might take. In the meanwhile, I wasn't going to impose myself on her when she had as much as asked me not to. So I was on my own.

But at least I found out how things stood. And I got rid of my demons, if not hers. I remembered the idea I had of her holding one wrist to her master and one to me, and passing on whatever ran through her. Now it felt as if I had broken the chain. I wasn't hooked anymore. She wasn't in me, and I wasn't in her. As the saying goes, I was in and out before I knew it.

I didn't have to think very hard about where I was going next. The horse's hooves went *thumpity-thump* as I crossed the bridge into Mexican town. I didn't have anything more to kick myself in the ass about, and my spirits lightened as I rode down the street toward Magdalena's house. It was early in the day. At a couple of houses in the *colonia*, women were sweeping off the doorsteps of their houses, and I wondered if Nena would be up yet.

She took a while coming to answer the

knock on the door, and I was afraid she might have company, but when she saw who I was, she opened the door and invited me in. Her voice was full of energy.

"Hello, Yimi. What's going on?"

"Not much, Nena. I finished with those people, so I came by here to say hello." I took off my hat and followed her into the living room.

"You finished?" She turned around.

"Yes, I did. It turns out that the evil fellow that was holding the girl was also the one that had my friend killed."

"The evil one? Not the hunchback?"

"No, his boss. The one called Melva."

"Oh, yes. I remember." Her green eyes widened. "So, did you have a fight?"

"Uh, yes."

"And the girl? Did she stay with him, then?"

I shook my head. "He's all done. But she stayed there anyway."

"Why, Yimi? Doesn't she like you, after all?"

"She has her troubles. Even with him out of the way, she's not free, and she has a lot of mending to do."

"Oh, I see. Well, everything falls by its own weight, doesn't it?"

"It seems to."

She gave me a soft smile. "Maybe you were lucky, Yimi. She would have given you too much trouble."

"Oh, I don't think she's that bad."

"Well, she changed her mind when she was here, after all the risks you took."

"She sure did that. And she did do it again."

"She was very nice, Yimi. But you know, someone who makes one basket will make a hundred."

"Maybe."

"I'm sorry. You're sad about it, aren't you?"

"Oh, not so much."

"Don't be sad. I think you're doing well not to get tied up with the girl. It's better this way. She's not the girl that is best for you."

"I think I feel sorry for her."

"Well, that's all right. And besides, she won't be alone forever."

"Oh, no. If she wants to see someone now, there won't be so much to keep her locked in."

"That's good. She's pretty, and she won't be without *pretendientes*."

"What's that?"

"A young man who comes by, and wants to try to see a girl and talk to her, and then he takes her out to go around."

I had a picture of Fernando, his face and boots all shiny, as he checked on the blondie girl. "I'm sure you're right," I said. "She won't be short on *pretendientes*."

"So everything will be fine, don't you think?"

"I suppose so."

I was getting a gradual look at Nena, and I could see she hadn't done herself up yet today. She hadn't put on lipstick and earrings, and her hair hung full and loose. She was wearing a plain brown dress, but she looked good all the way up and down.

"After all that," I said, "I'm not sure what I'm going to do next."

"In what way?"

"In all ways. I don't have a job, and I don't have a girl. Of course, I didn't have much of either before, I imagine."

"You can find a job."

"Oh, I'm sure."

"And a girl, too. There are different kinds." She flashed a smile. "What kind of a girl do you think you should have, Yimi?"

"I don't know. Sometimes I feel pretty stupid about it all."

"Do you think you should have someone nice, like my cousin Rosa Linda? She's gone now, but I use her for an example."

"Oh, I don't know if I'm ready for someone that nice, or if I will ever be."

"That's all right, too. You don't want to try for the wrong girl, whatever she is like."

"That's true."

"Why don't you just throw a little to the wind?" She seemed to be dancing even as she stood still.

"You mean, play?"

"I mean, don't be too serious. Do something that makes you feel good. Try to be free."

That was good advice. If there was someone a fellow would like to hear it from, it was Magdalena. She was one hell of a good girl.